George Mathews

Diary of a summer in Europe

1865

George Mathews

Diary of a summer in Europe
1865

ISBN/EAN: 9783337124403

Printed in Europe, USA, Canada, Australia, Japan

Cover: Foto ©Andreas Hilbeck / pixelio.de

More available books at **www.hansebooks.com**

DIARY

.

OF A

SUMMER IN EUROPE.

1865.

By PORTE.

———•———

NEW YORK:

MARSH'S PRINT, 110 DIVISION STREET.

——

1866.

NOTE.

... may be expected in reference to the contents of the following ...
... was written almost daily in those cities and regions where it purpo...
... solely for the future reference and satisfaction of the writer, and ...
... its ever being seen by any other than his own eye. But, as has ...
... was made (coming from a source not to be disregarded) that the ...
... ten out *just as they were taken*, though somewhat fuller. This re-
... as possible, complied with, and may account for any expressions ...
... med too personal, or too juvenile in their interpretation of the enthu-
... persons concerned. A further apology might perhaps be urged, in ...
... fact, that the first few pages of the Diary were written without ...
... that they were to be put into print even for private circulation ;
... been hastily prepared : and the latter portion during the unprece-
... sent summer.

S. P. W., JR.

DIARY.

Friday, June 23, 1865.—About 8 o'clock reached the side of the steamer "Lafayette," Capt. BOCANDE, accompanied by our friends; and for an hour were spectators of the usual scenes to be witnessed on the departure of an ocean-bound steamship. At 9 o'clock, precisely, the last farewells were spoken, and the plank, which was to separate some forever from those whom they loved, was lowered. Quietly we glided out upon the water, and were soon out of sight and hearing of those who had kindly accompanied us to the ship to wish us "bon voyage." And now it is evening, and our first day at sea is about ended. It has been a magnificent one: sea smooth, sky clear, and breeze refreshing. The deck has worn the aspect of the piazza of some summer resort; people of various ages and characters walking, sitting, reading and talking, and children running and romping about the vessel.

Sunday, June 25.—Notwithstanding we set sail on *Friday,* our voyage promises to be more than a "lucky" one. The sea continues calm, and the weather delightful. But it is not at all like Sunday. Some playing chess, others enjoying a game of cards, and the greater portion reading their novels. A few have their Bibles or books of religious poetry, but they are very few in number. Some of us have not slept much during the past two nights, owing to the novelty of our situation, and consequently feel much inclined to drowsiness. Up to the hour of noon, yesterday, we had made 248 miles, and to day at 12 o'clock had made 266 miles additional.

Monday, June 26,—Our table acquaintance, M. Cornelius De Boom, informed us this morning that during all his numerous voyages across the seas, he had never known such quiet, delightful weather, to continue for four consecutive days. Mrs. B. not inappropriately calls it "river sailing." Our sea life continues the same as may be seen from the following rhyme, which may pass for what it is worth.

On the "stormy Atlantic" this letter I rhyme,
And although done in part to wile away time,
I trust it will furnish some sort of idea
How we live, while across the ocean we steer.
The lives that we live are the lives of those men,
Who live for the present, nor labor to ken
The fears and the troubles the future may bring,
Living only for pleasure, and striving to fling
All saddening, sobering thoughts to the wind.

We sit upon deck, and pace o'er its floor ;
We talk, and we read, and list to the roar *
Of the wavelets, whose tops shine bright in the sun ;
As bright as the faces of children who run,
To and fro o'er the deck and serve to beguile
A dull hour, now and then, for those who can smile
Upon them, and thus win their young heart's affection,
And perchance from *their* spirits receive the reflection.

Lo here on the ocean, within a frail shell,
Four hundred inhabitants eat, drink and dwell !
Each and all of us strive to fill up our days
Just as we feel moved—in various ways—
The quiet people read, the social ones talk,
The wearied ones sleep and the restless ones walk ;
The idle ones lounge, and the dreamy ones smoke,
The ennuyed play cards and the funny ones joke,
And thus in one way and another all find
Employment of some sort for body and mind.

* The "roar of the wavelet" is not usually very loud.

Tuesday, June 27.—America is a thousand miles behind us! Still another superb day and sea almost as smooth as glass. EVENING—None of us dreamed this morning how eventful this day was to become! About 5 o'clock, just as we had finished our "second course" and were laughing and chatting over our dinners, the Captain disappeared from the table, and our attention was suddenly arrested by the exclamation of "a wreck! a wreck!" In a moment nearly every soul was on the deck, and all were straining their eyes to get a glimpse of "the wreck." We expected to see an old hull, or some blackened remnant of a ship; but we saw only a small row boat, rising and sinking again in the swell of the sea, as it made toward our ship. At first some of us were disappointed, but then came the realization that the little boat making toward our ship was a thousand miles from land, upon a treacherous sea and contained human beings who were, perhaps, famishing for want of food. The excitement caused by the agitation of several hundred people who running hither and thither to obtain a view of the approaching boat, may be more easily remembered by those of us who were eye-witnesses of the scene, and better imagined by those who were not—than described. Anxiously we waited for the little boat. At length it came alongside; the steps were lowered, and one by one the poor creatures were assisted to mount to the deck of the "Lafayette." No doubt it seemed to them as solid and safe as *terra firma*.

Their heart-rending tale was soon told. The ship "William Nelson," from Antwerp had been burnt the day before, about noon, hundreds had perished miserably, and these and a few others were all of the 500 souls on board the

ill-fated vessel who had been or would probably be saved.
They were taken to the second-class cabin and fed and
clothed. At first some were unable to taste food, so over-
joyed were they at their rescue from a watery grave;
while others were weeping for husbands and brothers
whom they should see no more. The passengers robbed
their own wardrobes for clothing to cover the poor creatures, many of whom were drenched to the skin. Later
in the evening a second boat load was received on board
the "Lafayette," and the Captain having ascertained the
location in which the ship was burned, changed his course
and sailed in a southerly direction. About dark we came
in sight of a Russian frigate, and about the same time de-
scried a third small boat quite near the vessel. Before we
came sufficiently near to speak the frigate she had received
the third boat's company on board. But all were subsequently transferred to the "Lafayette"; the whole number being 43 souls. There was something strange in this
intercourse on the ocean, and the transferrence of human
beings from one ship to another! Among those saved
were an entire family, father, mother and four children;
the youngest but three months old. The father said in his
own simple way, that "he did not know what he had
done to God that he should be so good to him." Why
were those few out of so large a company the only ones
saved? It may be they were to fulfill a destiny. It may
be we shall hear of some of them again. Until 11 o'clock
the Captain of our ship sailed in a southerly direction, and
at intervals fired rockets and cannon, hoping by these
means to attract the attention of any survivors who might
be floating about in the sea and thus save them from a
watery grave. But all in vain. The only response to the

booming of the cannon was the dull heavy feeling in our hearts.

Wednesday, June 28.—The thrilling scenes and incidents connected with the rescue occupy the thoughts and tongues of all on board, and we have more detailed accounts of the tragical scenes enacted before the eyes of those who were, two days ago, in the midst of the flames, which wrapt their vessel in a fiery shroud. In the afternoon there was a large assemblage of the passengers to witness the baptism of the youngest of all the survivors; an infant born upon the sea, and to whom was given the name of Lafayette Bocande, the names of the ship and Captain who saved him from a premature grave. Dr. King took the principal part in the unusual and touching scene, reading the baptismal service with great impressiveness, while our noble Captain held this child of the ocean in his arms. The weeping mother sat near, and at the close of the ceremony received and embraced the wondering and scarce conscious child. A subscription was then taken, and several thousand *francs* were collected by Madam Stoeckl, Judge Edwards Pierrepont and M. de'Boom, who had been appointed to act in the matter, and was distributed by them among the destitute passengers of the Nelson. Never was aid more spontaneously and gladly contributed, nor sympathy extended more heartily. Not raiment and gold alone were offered; but tears flowed for those sorrowing ones; they were visited in their loneliness and kind words were spoken to their aching hearts. We could not forget, that although the greatest boon of all, their lives, had been spared, yet they had lost those who were well nigh as dear to them as their own lives—their brothers, husbands, friends.

Monday, July 3.—We have passed a somewhat miserable day. Those who have been wishing for a storm have been gratified. The wind blows, the rain falls, and our vessel is rolling in a heavy sea. The initiated tell us it is not much of a storm; but those of us who have never before witnessed an upheaving of the ocean are somewhat incredulous. Only four or five ladies of the fifty on board presented themselves at the table, and not a few strong men are not to be found. Although not sick, (of course), our appetites were somewhat impaired, and a ship biscuit was sufficient to satisfy all cravings. All who were wise kept near as possible to the open deck, and diverted themselves by listening to the talk of others, yielding no attention to the claims of the inward man. The storm continued without abatement during the day. The dinner table presented the same dreary spectacle of deserted seats. For the first time since we started upon our voyage, the casings were put upon the table to prevent us from being drenched with claret, or having the contents of our plates diverted from their original destination. The greater portion of the company, however seemed more in danger of getting drunk than of taking much temperate food and drink, judging from the frequent calls upon the stewards for brandy and water—but necessity knows no law.

Tuesday, July 4,—The morning was so bright that its light struggled through the port holes, and we knew it was a " Glorious Fourth " before we reached the deck. But we had more substantial reason to remember the day, and proof that our good captain remembered it too. In more than one way was it celebrated, not only by champagne and speechifying but by the firing of cannon, and

the elevation of the stars and stripes to the masthead. And
was it not meet when the name of our vessel was " Lafayette" that the event, which the gallant Marquis had once
joined in celebrating, and for the consummation of which he
had fought, should be appropriately commemorated on this
particular day, when, after four years of sanguinary war
peace had dawned once more upon the land ! Be it as it
may, it was celebrated with a will. Young America inspired somewhat, it may be, by artificial stimulant cheered
the flag with much spirit, and sang in chorus a number of
patriotic airs. Nor was Captain Bocande forgotten. He
and other officers of the ship, were, in a double sense, *cor-
dially* remembered. Some of the toasts were, " The United
States," " France," " The Empereur" and " Bocande."
and so with the return of fine weather, the consciousness
that we were nearing our journey's end, and the hopes the
future held out to us we are all in good spirits.

Nine o'clock, P. M.—This day has been doubly celebrated ! Columbus, on his arrival at the new world saw a
light upon the land, although he could not see the land
itself. And we have seen a light on the shores of the old
world to-night ! It is as a star of promise and causes our
hearts to rejoice. It seems to be beckoning us onward,
assuring us that we are soon to realize the dream of years.

Wednesday, July 5th.—Evening. We have left the
ocean behind us ; have visited the harbor of Brest, where
some hundred or more passengers went ashore, and are
now steaming as rapidly as possible through the English
Channel for Havre. May God, who has in mercy piloted
us across three thousand miles of sea, grant us a safe arrival at the desired haven. We have enjoyed almost every

2

hour of our days on board, and shall not be as eager to leave
the ship as all would have been had we not experienced
an almost unparalelled succession of bright, beautiful
days, good company and good fare. Nevertheless we shall
be most glad to tread upon *terra firma* once more, and to
behold a new country.

Havre, July 6th, 2 P. M.—We can scarcely realize that
we are seated quietly in a veritable French hotel; that
time and steam have, in so brief a period, separated us so
widely from our homes. At ten we anchored in the channel, and about twelve stepped upon French territory, and
were soon afterward driven to the "Hotel de "Europa."
As we left the ship, the captain stood at the helm and
waved his chapeau, and the French flag was lowered to
the surface of the water, and raised to its place again, as a
final salute.

Good ship "Lafayette!" thou hast borne us safely over
the wide, wide sea, and we shall not soon forget thee.
May all who shall hereafter tread thy decks receive like
comfort, courtesy and safe transportation! As we passed
through "the gates," the people collected to see us land.
The soldiers were the exact counterpart, in appearance,
to the representations of them in the colored picture-
books we had so often seen at home. The houses, however, were entirely different, and prevent one from forget-
tin for a moment that he is in a foreign country. The
hotel is old, but the best; our rooms look into the little
paved court, from whence come the sound of the familiar
voices of many of our *compagnions du voyage*, commingled
with the lively clatter of the native tongue. The "Rue
de Paris," whereon the hotel is located, is a pleasant street,
lined with shops. Beneath one of the windows on the

opposite side of the street is painted in large Roman characters, of a yellow color, "English Spoken." But we shall do our shopping in Paris, whither we expect to go to-morrow, and only tarry here to see a friend, and collect our turbulent thoughts. The sun has shown constantly since our arrival. France has given us a bright reception.

Saturday, July 8th, a' Rouen.—What new and enjoyable sights, sounds, and experiences have been crowded into three short days! We have taken our first continental journey in the luxurious railroad carriages of the country—have seen the women at work in the fields—the old wooden windmills, and the thatched roofs of the mud houses. In this fine old city, which we had intended to leave unvisited, we have seen the spot whereon Joan of Arc was burned, the famous Hotel de Ville, a gloomy pile of brick and stone, and other places which demand especial mention. Having examined the exterior of several of the principal public buildings, we drove to the Church of St. Ouen, where we spent an hour in viewing pictures of various merit—in studying the grand yet delicate architecture of this magnificent edifice—in looking at the beautiful stained glass windows, and in contemplating the church as a whole. The major-domo who conducted us through the building aided us considerably to obtain a just conception of its size and beauty. The enclosed altar was too sacred a place for the feet of heretics; but we went into many of the little side chapels, in most of which were confessionals. A picture in one of them was worthy of attention. It was a representation of the devil; the form, part man and part serpent, and the face so fascinating as to rivet the attention of the beholder. How much thought, labor and gold have been bestowed to render the false attractive, and uphold a superstitious worship! Before we left, we were told to look into a fount of water, in which the church was mirrored. Of course it looked "up side down ;" but an opportunity was afforded of observing the arched ceiling without the danger of dislocating one's neck. We shall ever recollect with enthusiasm our visit to this grand old cathedral of St. Ouen of Rouen. To our mind, the Notre Dame, which is "*the* cathedral" of the city, is not so impressive, and the architecture is more heavy and sombre. At the time we visited it, workmen were engaged in making repairs, and their presence and noise detracted somewhat from the interest the edifice would otherwise have inspired.

In the afternoon we took a carriage to Mt. St. Catherine, on an eminence of which stands the new, handsome Church of the Lady of Bonsecours. The interior is extremely dazzling. The magnificent storied windows, which were given by the donors whose names and likenesses adorn one corner of them, form an important part of the whole. The painting and gilding is of the most gorgeous description, and the church is altogether one of the gayest places for worship of any kind that we have ever seen.

As much, if not more than the inspection of this church, did we enjoy the superb view of the valley of the Seine, including the town of Rouen, and several small hamlets. Looming up in the midst of the town was seen the tower of the Cathedral, surmounted by the iron spire which, from its great height, seemed to cleave the low clouds which were at the time moving rapidly over the city ; while below, the river winding through the picturesque valley, and studded with woody islands, enhanced the beauty of the scene. Long will the picture be retained in our memory !

July 9th, Sunday.—Attended grand mass at the Notre Dame. We reached the cathedral just as the priests were marching through the aisles, chanting a part of the service as they walked, and elevating the cross between the lighted candlesticks. This ceremony over, the Romish service commenced : kneeling to the Holy Virgin, praying, putting on and off of robes and caps, reading the Latin Lessons, swinging the incense, and so forth. Wearied with the monotonous tones of the priests, we found more profit in giving heed to the sober reflections called forth by the sight of all these pompous performances. The throng who filled the church also afforded an interesting subject for contemplation ; while many, it could not be doubted, were sincere worshipers ; others, while pretending to be engaged in petitioning the blessed Mary, were taking cognizance of all that was going on about them. But the Catholics are not the only ones who carry on the worship of God and mammon at one and the same time. We took, but did not partake of, the sacrament, wrapping the bit of bread (which was, in the belief of those around us, a particle of the body of the Saviour) in one corner of our pocket handkerchief. We bore it away with us as a sensible proof of our *unbelief* in the doctrine of transubstantiation, and as a memento of the service— the first we had attended in the old world ! We remained to witness the " public prayers to the Virgin." While they were being mumbled with the accustomed formal solemnity, a French woman entered, whom we recognized as having been a passenger on board the La- fayette. The expression of her face was not particularly amiable, and we wondered at the facility with which, while, with one closed eye, she adored the "Holy Mother," she with the other cast a severe glance upon us, as if to reprove us for want of due reverence. It was refreshing to get out into the pure air and sunshine once more; and still more so—after an interval of several hours passed quietly in our pleasant rooms in the Hotel D'Angleterre—to attend the English Episcopal service in a little chapel which was once a Catholic church. It was situated in a most out-of-the-way place; and had we been persecuted Huguenots it would have been seemingly a safe retreat. All directions were of no avail; and had it not been for a very polite shopman, who insisted upon leaving his shop, and going far out of his way, we should not have enjoyed this heretical service. About forty were assembled, and joined heartily in the responses; and some four or five fair American or English girls sat near the small melodeon, and with their sweet voices aided materially in rendering the vocal part of the service attractive. Owing to the fewness of our numbers, and the circumstances under which we worshiped, there seemed more than usual union and communion. We felt that it was good to be there and to pause for a moment in the midst of the excitements incident to the life of a traveler journeying through a country where all things were new and strange.

Monday, July 10th,—Left Rouen, not without some regret, and by two o'clock were on our way to Paris! The ride of two hours and a half was very enjoyable, the country through which we passed attractive,, and our spirits the finest. There is much to engage the attention of one who gazes upon the region of country through which this road passes for the first time in their lives. What struck us particularly as we proceeded was the singular custom of cultivating the soil, in immensely long and very narrow strips; each strip having been planted with a different kind of produce, and presenting a marked appearance, and looking like a great agricultural flag, with its many colored and variously shaded stripes, spread upon the surface of the ground. The train in which we were being conveyed to the capitol of " Le Belle France," also attracted our attention, the cars being covered with sheet iron without, and illumined by means of a lamp placed in the centre of the top and lighted by a man upon the roof! There is also no shelter whatever upon the engine for the fireman who drives it. Many other of the arrangements differ widely from our own, as for instance the rate of speed which being far greater, is certainly much more agreeable, especially when one's destination is this paradise of pleasure seekers. As we neared the city our excitement increased, and even when we had passed the *barriere* we could scarcely believe the testimony of our senses, that we were not beside ourselves, but were in very truth *in Paris* !

The examination of our baggage was little more than a form, and after a very brief delay, with our trunks over our heads upon the top of little *voiture*, we were getting our first actual sight of the gay city while being driven to the Boulevard des Capucins, and " le Grand Hotel." Owing to the impossibility of carrying all our luggage upon one coach, our party was obliged to separate, and the *cocher* of one of the the *voitures* conjecturing rightly as to the ignorance of his passenger or " voyageur" as to the rout to be taken, gave him the benefit of half an hour's ride through various portions of the city, thus enabling him, in advance of his *compagnons*, to gain a knowledge of its beauty and magni-

tude.   Considering the advantages thus unexpectedly
enjoyed, the trifling extra charge which was exacted was
very inconsiderable.

Unlike many of the little "grands" to which the attention of the traveler is constantly invited, this palatial
hotel is most appropriately named.   In size and all its
appointments it has not its equal, and certainly not its
superior in certain other important respects.   We were
soon established in most comfortable quarters, and ere
long found our way to a handsome restaurant, where we
were waited upon by *garcons* clothed in fine broadcloth,
and speaking three or four languages, and where we enjoyed a most satisfactory repast.

In the evening, by moonlight, as if in a vision, we
looked upon the Madeleine, the Place de la Concorde, with
its obelisk of Luzor, the exterior of the Palace of the Tuilleries; and after a short stroll through the corridors of
the Rue Rivoli, returned to our rooms.   We had had excitement enough for one day; and what promise did not
the morrow hold out to us!

Paris, July 13*th.*—On first entering the city, we were
forced to exclaim, "O strange new world!" and indeed the
intense life and brilliancy of the "whited sepulchre" cannot
be easily described.   There is an intense sparkle and fascination about it that one must himself witness in order
to understand it.   Three days in Paris constitute an event
in one's lifetime; that is, to one coming from the New
World.   What have we not done, seen, experienced even,
during so brief a time!   We have been lost amid the curious and interesting treasures of art and antiquity stored
in the Louvre; fine old pictures, souvenirs of the kings

and queens of France, (beginning with Childric and ending with Louis Philippe,) and articles of all descriptions used by Napoleon the Great—have visited the tombs of Abelard and Heloise, Rachael, Marshal Ney, and the Rothschilds, at Pere la Chaise—have been through the manufactory of the Gobelin Tapistry, where we were much entertained by a view of the finished pieces, the work of years, and wonderful specimens of art, and by watching the process by which they are constructed, *thread by thread.* We have seen the Jardin des Plantes, where we looked upon many animals never before collected. The Morgue—although at the time of our visit there were none but living inhabitants within the walls—claimed a moment's attention. Next we visited "Notre Dame de Paris," so intimately connected with the history of the city. Walking up the side aisles, and noticing the side chapels which had been repaired and adorned, we looked at the beautiful carved work within the chancel, and returned and climbed the left tower to the first "look-out;" then, crossing to the right-hand tower, climbed to the very top, and, scrambling upon the roof, stood upon the highest attainable point. From this elevation the view of the immense and finely-situated city, extending far out into the region round about, was grand in the extreme.

Our visit to the Invalides, to-day, was a very interesting one. Bonaparte's tomb is very rich, and the statues surrounding it finely executed and commanding. The building itself is very handsome, and, altogether, impressive. We afterward spent a short time in the hospital itself, its chapel, etc. Driving past the magnificent Arc de l'Etoile, after examining its fine bass-relief, we went to the Luxomborg Palace, its senate chamber, gallery of paintings,

and so forth. The gallery of paintings was worthy of a
much longer visit. Indeed some of the paintings merited
an hour's inspection ; and supposing the inspector to possess a good memory and a fertile imagination, the examination might afford much delightful thought and enjoyment.

From the Palace we went to the Pantheon, a famous
old church, on its own and its historical account. Guided
by a hearty, merry-looking man, habited in the usual dress
of the military order, we descended into the vaults beneath
the altar, and visited the tombs of Voltaire, (the man
whose character Carlyle has so admirably drawn,) and
Rousseau, and some other notabilities. At one spot our
guide stopped, and, arranging us in a row, with our backs to
the wall, stepped onward a little distance, and pronounced
a number of words—at first in a loud, and then in a softer
tone, which were re-echoed with a precision such as we
had never known to be equalled or even approximated.
The whispered ones were as distinct as the louder ones.
He next sounded a drum, and the noise which resounded
from the vaults and arches was like the roar of artillery.
Our courier afterward informed us that the drum used
was quite a small one. Close by the Pantheon stands the
oldest church in Paris, St. Genevieve. In the revolution
it was used as a stable, and was the theatre of some fight-
ing. Several bullet-holes, which were shown to us in the
canvass of some of the paintings, testified to the truth of
the event.

Our last visit was to the Chamber of Deputies, where
we saw the room in which the deputies assemble. A fine
marble statue of the present Emperor was greatly ad-

mired. It is cut from a single block of marble, and is most beautifully and perfectly executed.

It seems, that while so much has met our eyes, our minds have been inadequately employed. One feels the momentary impression, but does not analyze the cause whence it comes; and consequently he fails to derive the full pleasure and profit which might be received by a cooler and more lengthened study, both of his thoughts and the works of art themselves.

In the evening, as usual, strolled in the Boulevards, sometimes visiting the arcades and passages, looking at the display of goods which the French people know how to arrange so temptingly in their shop-windows, and occasionally purchasing some trifling articles. In thus making ourselves, for the time being, one of the easily-pleased throng, and sauntering leisurely whither inclination led us, we found much entertainment; and although the occupation yielded no excitement, it afforded no small opportunity to observe the street life, shop life, and common life of the gay city—to study " Paris by gaslight."

July 14th, Versailles.—Left in the half-past eleven o'clock train for Versailles. The ride of less than an hour's duration was only too short. Driving through the long avenue, lined on either side with a double row of fine trees, we reached the little Trianon, and so soon as the officer arrived, were shown through its apartments. Many of them were very elegant. The floors being of inlaid wood, and highly polished, seemed no more fit to be trodden upon than the handsome centre-tables that adorned the rooms, and upon which were arranged many unique and valuable gifts presented to Napoleon First by the sove-

reigns of Europe.   Beyond these more showy *salons*, we
passed through the sitting-room, private library, bed-
chamber, and toilet-room of Bonaparte, and saw likenesses
of various members of the old Bourbon family.

Next in order came the inspection of the royal livery.
Among the carriages, was the one in which the young
prince was carried at the time of his christening, and the
coach in which Josephine was sent away from her lawful
husband.   All were richly ornamented, and gorgeous with
gilt.   We also saw the chair in which Madame Maintenon,
the fascinating woman of society, was carried.

To pass through the galleries of the Grand Palace of
Versailles occupied several hours ; and it would be utterly
impossible to describe either the magnificent *Palaise* itself, or
to name its most valuable treasures.   Most of the paintings
relate to great historical events and battle-fields, and the
sculpture to men who have made themselves famous or
infamous in history.   One wearies of the multitude of objects claiming his attention, and is bewildered by the
splendor and elaborateness of the pictures, as well as the
rooms in which they are arranged.

Sunday, July 16th.—We have been to church almost
daily since we landed—but to pay homage to art and antiquity.   To-day we went to worship God.   In the little
American chapel, Rue de Berri 21, we joined in a service
partly Presbyterian, partly Episcopal, and wholly in English.   We listened to a somewhat rambling discourse from
Dr. S.   His subject was one offering a wide field for
imaginative display ; but his treatment of it was eminent-
ly practical.   It was the raising of Lazarus from the dead ;
and the striking thought was, that Christ, by this act of
love and mercy, hastened the event of his crucifixion.

Mainly, pleasure is God in this magnificent city ; and the thought will come, whether these gay Parisians would not be quite ready to crucify the Lord again, should he come among them, and endeavor to raise them to a higher, nobler life. Where were the three million inabitants of the city ? Traveling, selling goods, building houses, and a few praying to the Virgin.

Monday, July 17th.—A fourth excessively warm day. Drove out of Paris a few miles to visit the famous church of St. Denis, where so many of the kings and queens of France are buried. The church is being repaired, so that we were able to see only a small part of it. Notwithstanding Bonaparte's desire to " sleep on the banks of the Seine, in the midst of the French people," the present Emperor designs that his remains shall be entombed amidt the walls wherein the skeletons of the ancient nobility of the empire are buried. And it is by his order that the stonecutters are at work within the hallowed walls. But we were repaid for our visit ; the building itself, excepting the portion destroyed by lightning some years ago, is 1,200 years old ! and the multitudinous associations that cluster around it, render it an object of awe and intense interest to a lover of history or one who reverences antiquity.

Before returning home we drove to the Bourse, the magnificent railroad depot of the " Nord" roads, the old church of St. Eustache, the Palais Royal, the markets, and the Bank of France. The roar of what, to the uninitiated, might seem more like the raving of a multitude of maniacs, which greeted our ears as we entered " la Bourse," was almost deafening. This is a handsome and commanding edifice, and occupies a fine position. The markets are fine structures of iron, and admirably suited for the reception of the eatables therein sold. We have nothing like them at home; but it would be for the health of the people if we had. Before leaving, we bought some delicious fruit, which we brought home to refresh ourselves therewith when thirsty or faint. Spent the evening in the delightful Salon de Lecture of the hotel over the London " *Times*." Read about the Atlantic cable—which it seems is just about to be laid again, with new hopes and improvements—the burning of the Nelson, some of whose passengers we picked up; and last, but not least, *several columns on America*, feeling complimented the while that my native land merited so much notice in so great a paper. We had scarcely looked at a paper for weeks, and nothing but indisposition and a thirsting for home-knowledge, could have induced us to remain within to-night.

Wednesday, July 19th,—It is a week since we commenced to "do" Paris seriously, and we have been surprised to learn how much we could examine (not merely *pass by*) in a day, under the auspices of a courier familiar with the city, and its treasures of art, beauty and antiquity. Paris is unexhausted, inexhaustible, but is intensely hot; and so having engaged a passage in the Scotia, of October 7th, we are off for Switzerland and Germany to-morrow.

July 21st, Geneva.—Yesterday morning we left Paris, and rode for nine hours through the southeast portion of the empire of France. It was somewhat tedious, but we enjoyed seeing the country through which we journeyed. The highly-cultivated, fenceless fields—the hedges by the side of the track—the beautiful hillsides, checkered with different kinds of grain or vegetables—the women working as hard as the men—(we did *not* enjoy this)—the aged look of the houses, and so forth. It stormed a part of the time; but we were enabled to see all that was to be seen without interruption. About half-past eight we reached Macon, where we slept all night. At eight o'clock this morning in the rain we left the little, stagnant, dismal town, in the way train, and were consequently obliged to travel slowly, wait for trains at intermediate stations, and change carriages a number of times. The latter part of our ride was through narrow defiles, between high hills, and the scenery possessed more variety than that of yesterday. But we did not see it to as much advantage; for, although in one of the best carriages, we were, for the first time since our arrival, somewhat crowded. All annoyances were, however, soon forgotten; for presently we were in Switze. land! Arrived at Geneva, we went at once to the Hotel des Bergnes, which, though not new, is, like old wine, good; and moreover, is said to command a view of Mt. Blanc in clear, cloudless weather. He has not been visible to-day. After dinner—which, by the way, was enlivened by music from a fine band—we passed over the handsome bridge across the lower end of the lake, and into some of the older portions of the city.

July 22d, Chamonix.—Left the Hotel Bergues for this little Alpine village about eight and a half o'clock. We accomplished eighteen miles of the journey in less than three hours, and at Bonnville remained more than an hour to rest the horses. At the same time and place we refresh- ed ourselves, though in a small way. We were on the way again a little after twelve, and did not stop until two hours afterward, when the horses were again rested; and meanwhile a cannon fired that we might hear the echo. It was poor, and by no means equal to the one at Lake George. During the ride thence to St. Martin, we passed some beautiful scenery, and very lofty mountain tops. All was new, wild, grand and strange, and we forgot the length of the journey, in witnessing the novel and impressive scenery, by which we were surrounded. About half-past three we reached the inn of St. Martin, and here we changed coaches, drivers and horses, to ascend the mountain which formed the barrier to the village to which we were bound. A part of the traces connecting the horses with our new conveyance were made of pieces of rope, not larger than a common clothes line, and seemed scarcely to warrant safe transportation up the sides of the steep ascent. However, we journeyed up the steep sides of the wild mountain and over bridges thrown across yawning chasms in safety, even to the end. About seven, we beheld the snowy peaks of the mountains in the neighborhood of Mt. Blanc ; but it was not until we neared the village that the clouds were lifted from the tops of the mountains, at the base of which ran our road, and from the hoary head of this giant king of the Alps, that we looked upon the very top of the world-famous Mount Blanc ! Yes, there it was, looming up into the very sky, and we, mere pigmies, straining our eyes and almost dislocating our necks to gaze at it. We were informed that people are frequently a week at Chamonix, and do not get one glimpse of this dazzling monarch, and that we were fortunate ; and indeed we thought so too, and felt awed when we thought of our proximity to those fearful glaciers, and the cloud-enveloped regions where the snow eternally rests and perpetual silence reigns !

Sunday, July 23d.—On our arrival last evening, we had found rest at the Hotel Royal, which was honored in 1860 by a visit from the French Emperor and suite. The rooms assigned us commanded a view of the snow-topped summits, and consequently the *first* thing we did upon rising was to go to our windows to see if the sky was clear. To our joy it was, and the round, pure, crystal dome of Mt. Blanc was glistening in the sunlight! About eleven, leaving the hotel, we moved leisurely along the little field-path leading to the newly-erected Episcopal chapel, lately built to accommodate English tourists. We were very early, as the village time differed from our own. Soon, however, the little bell was tolled, and the people began to come; and by the time the service commenced, the very small church was well filled. It seemed fit to worship the Author of all the sublimity which surrounded us in the midst of his creations—" to lift up our eyes unto the hills, from whence cometh our help;" unto Him "who has preserved us from all evil," during the month that has elapsed since we left our homes on the other side of the Atlantic. If, indeed, there are " sermons in stones—books in the running brooks," what depths of thought may not be stirred within one by giving heed to the emotions caused by a contemplation of these grand phenomena of nature. It makes the spectator feel his insignificance, question the very cause of his creation, and yearn for some imagined, inexpressible good. A memorable day will be this Sabbath, passed under the "Shadow of Mount Blanc!"

July 24th.—Well was it that we took a long, last look at Mt. Blanc last evening; for to-day his glorious head is

4

no longer visible to the gaze of mortals. The event of the
day was the ascent to the Mer de Glace, on mule-back. It
occupied about two hours. B. was mounted on the back
of the largest animal, myself upon the most mischievous.
They were "stubborn as mules," and it was well for us
that they had made up their minds that they *would* go.
They went no faster than they chose, however, and occasionally paused to view their homes beneath, or for some other
undiscovered reason. Now and then the road became un-
pleasantly narrow, and ran uncomfortably near to something very like a precipice; and just at these points the
donkeys seemed especially desirous of seeing how close to
the edge they could walk without causing themselves
and their riders to make an unexpected descent. However, we reached the plateau overlooking the Sea of Ice—
regarding the extent and appearance of which we were a
little disappointed—in safety, and drank our bottle of
beer several thousand feet above the heads of most of our
fellow men. Descending part way to the icy sea, we
watched a party of young men, as, with pikes in their
hands, and conducted by a guide, they threaded their
way across it; and then, not having time to cross ourselves, we bought some exquisite wood carvings, as mementoes of our visit, and commenced the not quite so
agreeable descent. It was accomplished in good time;
and about four, with regret, we bade adieu to the moun-
tain-locked vale of Chamonix, and descended to the little
inn at St. Martin, where we intended passing the night, in
order to lessen the fatigue of the return to Geneva on the
morrow. It was worth the journey across the Atlantic,
we thought, this visit to Mt. Blanc alone.

July 27th—Berne to Brienz.—Having been entertained
by the Alpine views, the bears, and the wonderful music
boxes of Berne, we started this morning for Interlaken
The sail through the beautiful lake of Thun was very enjoyable. It occupied about an hour. We had not been
upon the water before since leaving the Lafayette, (the
great fête at Veray having prevented our contemplated
sail through the lake of Geneva,) and it was most refreshing to feel the cool breeze, and breathe the exhilarating
air, as we sat upon the deck of the miniature steamer,
viewing the emerald setting of this gem-like lake. At
Neauhaus, we found stages waiting the arrival of the
boat, and were rapidly conveyed to Interlaken, a beautifully and most romantically situated summer resort.
Here we dined, and passed several hours at the Belve-
dere. We found the people talking of the terrible acci-
dent of the Metterhorn, whereby young Lord Douglass
and two of his companions lost their lives. To our
regret, the " Jungfran " was not visible. Neither were
the friends we sought; and therefore, having engaged
a private conveyance to Lucerne, we drove as far as
Brienz, on the lake of the same name. It was a
small inn at which we stopped, situated on the edge of
the water, and the windows of our rooms were delightfully located, looking out upon the little mountain-bound
lake, with the famous falls of Giesbach tumbling down
the mountain on the opposite side. How we wished, as
our eyes took in the grand and beautiful picture, that
those who had gone from this world could have looked
upon these enchanting scenes ! Yet, may they not be in
a world where all is far more beautiful than aught that is
here ? After we had partaken of some rest and refresh-

ment, we crossed the lake in a rowboat, in " pitch darkness" and a drizzling rain, to visit the falls. It took us
an hour to cross the lake, and ascend half way to the top
of the height over which the water is precipitated. Meanwhile the rain increased, and the single lantern carried by
the guide was scarcely sufficient to show us the path
leading up the ascent through the forest; but when,
after waiting impatiently for some fifteen minutes, the
illumination took place, we forgot everything in beholding
the magical spectacle. The cascade of water seemed in a
moment transformed into a cascade of flaming fire, of various hues, red, blue, green, and yellow. Viewed in the
surrounding " blackness of darkness," it almost seemed as
if we were permitted to look into the region where the
Stygian river overflowed its banks! We could scarcely
talk of aught else but the illuminated falls of Giesbach,
and of the surprise and delight experienced when the impressive spectacle suddenly burst upon our vision, while
descending the mountain and recrossing the lake to the
hotel.

Friday, July 28th.—Brienz to—nowhere. Resumed our
journey to Lucerne this morning. Crossed the Brenig
mountain. About two, stopped at a wayside inn to dine
and feed the horses. The morning had been so excessively warm as even to impair our enjoyment of the extra-
ordinary scenery which Sir Walter Scott has so graphic-
ally depicted in " Anne of Geierstein." About two indi-
cations of a storm appeared. Two hours later we were
again on our way, and not long after the rain began to
fall—slowly at first, but by-and-by in torrents. Pausing
under a covered bridge, which fortunately was near at
hand, we waited till the worst was over, and continued

our journey, until a mountain torrent, which had washed away a portion of the road, precluded further progress. Back we went to an inn not far distant, and waited for the torrent to run out. In half an hour thereafter, by the help of half a dozen men, the carriage was brought over the stones, and through the water which was rushing and foaming across the road. It was at the risk of being overturned, and having the carriage broken, that we passed; and scarcely had the passage been accomplished, when a similar break in the highway appeared. But we again succeeded in passing, and all went well until we arrived at a point where a bridge had been carried away by the flood. Owing, however, to the energy of our driver, who pulled off his coat, and went to work with a will—thus inspiring those who were listlessly looking on, without a thought, apparently, of laboring to repair the damage done to work also—the delay was brief, and soon our own and several other vehicles were safely on the other side of the foaming stream.

We were destined to have an adventurous time. Proceeding only a short distance, we reached a second bridge-less, rushing rivulet, likewise impassable. But again it was repaired, and we went a little farther, when we came to a place where the effects of the severe and—as the Swiss peasants informed us—unparalled storm was visible in piles of earth and stone thrown across the entire passage. All got out, and walked over on foot, and on came the carriage, pitching from side to side, and being with difficulty brought over by any means. Farther on, the windows of our conveyance, almost brushed against the gnarled trunk of an immense tree, which had been uprooted by the tempest and overturned upon the road, leaving scarcely room

to pass between it and the Lake of Lucerne, upon the
edge of which ran the road. Truly, the storm had been
"abroad in the mountains!" and there had been "war in
the skies." We began to realize that our position was not
only fearful, but, as M. Varlet, our courier, exclaimed,
"*perfectly fearful.*" Still, the excitement kept off fear,
although the thought that some huge tree or boulder
might be precipitated upon our pitiless heads was not at
all a pleasant one. For aught we knew, we might be
buried alive. All agreed we would not "stage" it among
the Alps again in a storm—and especially not on
Friday.

Hoping, notwithstanding the difficulties which lay in
our path, that we should before nightfall reach the town
to which we were destined, we did not despair, though conscious that our ride was a dangerous one, from what we
had seen. This was not to be, however. When within a
mile of Lucerne, we reached a part of the road where
earth, logs and stones had been piled in promiscuous confusion, and to a considerable height. But, by skillful
manœuvring, we might have passed even this spot, had
not a knowledge of the insurmountable obstacles a few
feet beyond precluded all thought of completing the journey, although within a mile and a half of the town.

A little drinking tavern was at hand, and, by means of
chairs and boards, we were enabled to reach the steps
thereof dry-shod. The road was flooded in all directions,
and it was even difficult to effect a "landing" for the
carriage. We were not alone in our discomforture. A
party who had been traveling close behind us were in a
like situation, and found shelter for the night and from
the storm under the same roof. Our company was fur-

ther increased by the addition of two young German lads, who were making a pedestrian tour through the region. The kind people gave up their own rooms and beds, (the latter were not in all cases used,) and sent to the nearest village to get butter and eggs, and did all in their power to comfort and oblige us. All the members of our party appropriated the dining room to themselves, lying down upon the sofas, tables and chairs. But we slept, nevertheless.

July 29th.—We rose at an unusually early hour, hoping to take a row-boat from the point where we were, and thereby reach the town without being obliged to retrace our steps; but the old scow, the only conveyance securable, was not fit; and so we went in our carriage to Stanstadt, and waited for the little steamer which was to leave at nine for Lucerne. As we rode through the village in the pure, refreshing morning air and sunshine, we saw the devastating effects of the storm of last evening, in the desolate-looking hillsides, where the torrent, rushing down the mountain, had loosened and carried away trees, turf and rocks, and had, in a few hours, buried the gardens and the carefully cultivated fields upon which the poor Switzers had bestowed many days of hard labor. The little lake steamer was punctual to a moment, and with passengers and baggage (an unusual amount of both) on board, we were soon gliding through the water towards the beautifully-situated, though not otherwise prepossessing, town of Lucern. In about three-quarters of an hour we reached the landing, and were soon luxuriating in the Schweitzerhof, in rooms commanding a delightful view of the lovely lake, the Rigi, and other blue-topped mountains·

After paying a satisfactory visit to the handsome marble
dining hall, we strolled through a part of the town, crossing the old bridge, with its curious, old and faded pictures,
and winding about through some of the narrow, dark
streets of the town. Later, after a drive into the country,
over the fine hard road, and in view of the grand heights,
we visited the sculpture of the "Lion," after the celebrated model of Thorwalsden, executed in commemoration of the death of the gallant Swiss Guard. It is a
marvelous production, and he must be a callous man who
can view it unmoved. Art is grand, but nature is often
more powerful to stir the depths of one's whole nature.
We were in the midst of *moving* scenes in more than in
one sense. The wondrous panorama was constantly
changing under the influence of the golden-tinted sunset
clouds which were reflected in the waters of the unruf-
fled lake, and the scenery at once so quiet and grand, and
exceedingly beautiful, as to melt the heart, and bring
back, with powerful vividness, all those tender scenes and
associations of the past which few have not experienced
during life's journey, and the remembrance of which bring
tears to the eyes of the beholder.

July 31st.—Out of Switzerland—into Germany. About
ten we left our last resting-place in this land of unrivalled
grandeur, sublimity and beauty, for Baden-Baden. The
scenery changed gradually, though perceptibly, after
leaving Lucerne, and we took a last, lingering look at the
partially-obscured mountains, thinking, with more than
regret, that it would probably be our last. We had
passed a delightful Sabbath on the shores of the lovely
lake, giving thanks for our deliverance from the perils of

the storm by which we had been overtaken, and drinking deeply of the pure and elevating enjoyments peculiar to our situation in this unequalled region. A cloud, though not much bigger than a hand's bredth, resting upon the Rigi, had rendered the ascent of that height unadvisable; and so, disappointed, but filled with thrilling recollections of this enchanting land, we journeyed on. Certainly *this* world is surpassingly beautiful, and induces us too often to forget the existence of another. But that other must, in truth, be wonderful, if, notwithstanding all there is to enrapture one here, " it hath not entered into the heart of man to conceive" its glories! O, Switzerland! what man who has crossed thy mountains, beheld thy vallies, floated upon thy lakes, witnessed the descending storm and torrent within thy borders, can for a moment wonder that thine inhabitants love thee? and that, if perchance they are forced to seek a foreign home, where no lofty mountain-tops reach up into the sky, pine for thee; and after years of toil come back to enjoy thy grandeur? Wild and beautiful—terrible and fascinating—thou art a land to influence and control the soul of man, as is none other. Farewell!

At Barle we passed out of Switzerland and into Germany The examination of our baggage was slight, and ere long we were crossing the Rhine(!) and passing over the plains and by the dykes of Germany. The contrast between this scenery and that in the midst of which we were but a few hours since was indeed extreme. It was about seven when we reached this great and fashionable pleasure resort, and too tired, dusty and hungry to commence sight-seeing, or to attend the grand musical *fete* held that evening in the " Conversation," we walked through some of the

streets, and returned to the "L'Europe" where we were
lulled to sleep by the sounds of the music coming from the
not far distant hall.

August 1st—Baden-Baden.—The first thing to be done
after leaving one's room in the morning, is to visit the
"Drinkerhalle," where the mineral waters are taken, and
where on showery mornings one has a good opportunity
afforded for pre-breakfast exercise, and seeing the "invalids," many of whom present the appearance of robust
jollity, if not wicked joility. But most interesting to be
seen and enjoyed is the ride and visit to the Castle of the
Margraves, which has for so long a time been in ruins. We
spent some time in rambling over the remains of the fortress, and from the top of the only tower left standing had
a fine view of the surrounding country. By means of a
good telescope, several distant towns on the borders of the
Rhine are brought within the vision, and even some of the
buildings within those towns. When about half-way down
the mountain we stopped to inspect the Palace of the present Duke of Baden, but were permitted to see only two or
three rooms in the main building, as the Duchess was within
the walls; but descending into the region of perpetual night,
in company with several other visitors, each of us having
been furnished with a lamp, we followed the guide through
the dungeons where, not three hundred years ago, deeds of
great cruelty were perpetrated; and as we listened to these
tales of horror, congratulated ourselves that we had not
been born dukes in those days, and in that neighborhood.

Having returned from the dark ages and the gloom of
midnight into the glorious light of noonday, we enjoyed
one of those charming drives through a park-like portion

of the town, beneath a fine avenue of trees, whose branches meeting above our heads, afforded a most refreshing shade, and beneath the bows of which, on either side of the road, were romantic vistas, rustic seats, and lounging invalids. Some of the latter were really infirm, and were being moved through the grounds by servants in wheeled chairs or carriages; while others, perchance, were killing time by talking scandal, or reading the latest novel.

In the afternoon we found amusement in examining the contents of the booths or small shops ranged around a large square in the neighborhood of the *Conversation*. They were attended by people from a dozen different countries, and the display of goods was as various as the productions of the regions from whence they came. The shopkeepers were remarkably polite; but whether it was from respect to ourselves, or on account of divers trifling purchases made, it would be difficult to determine.

While dining at the *table d'hote*, we were furnished, for two kreutzers, with a list of visitors in the place, (which is published daily,) and were amused to find the announcement of the arrival of one of our party " mit bed." Not being acquainted with the signification of the term, and being not at all desirous to have the property of some invalid traveler accounted as our own, we were not a little puzzled, until informed that reference was had to the courier who accompanied us! Dinner over with hundreds of fellow sojourners, we secured seats fronting the handsome hall, listened to the fine inspiriting music of the band, and watched the gay throng of pleasure-seekers. The change of mood produced upon the people by the varied music without, answered to the exciting freaks of fortune and clink of gold, which alternately agitated those at the gaming table within the *Conversation*. We visited the hall between the hours of nine and ten, and watched the players and the game. It was a sad though fascinating spectacle, and finished our sight-seeing for the day.

August 2d.—Baden-Baden to Frankfort. About half-past eleven o'clock we left Baden-Baden, the fashionable and extremely picturesque watering-place of the world, for Frankfort-on-the-Main. Journeying for a time through the region of the Black Forest, we found much to admire and delight the eye, and were enjoying all the pleasure and excitement incident to a first ride on the German railway, when the arrival of the train at Bruchsal Junction put an end to our enjoyment for a longer period than the time-being, and brought the blackness of darkness upon our spirits—making this journey one which will be forever memorable. We learned (through Dr. Dodge, of N. Y., who was journeying in the same train with ourselves) that one, who had but a few weeks since, with a beaming face waved us a glad adieu as we sailed away from our native land, and who who was then in the full flush of budding manhood, had sickened, died and (ere we knew that he was ill) been buried. Even as the intense heat of summer withers and kills the young plant, so had a virulent fever destroyed the vitality and burned up the life of him whom we were to see no more. Still we journeyed on, one in sympathy—well nigh one in feeling—unmindful of scenes which no longer had power to attract our gaze, excite our imagination, and awaken new and varied interest—we thought only of those dear ones who had gone "the way of all the earth," and would ne'er welcome us back with joy when all our wanderings are o'er. We scarcely knew whether we were not, even yet, travelling through the "Black Forest," so utterly had all enthusiasm departed from our souls, and so very dark was the cloud that rested upon our spirits. By nightfall we reached the end of our day's pilgrimage, and after driving to several hotels, all of which were crowded to their utmost capacity, we at length obtained most comfortable quarters in the Hotel of the Roman Emperor.

August 4th—Frankfort.—Nature seems often to sympathize with nations, as, when during a protracted war, the dull, heavy, threatening clouds have for days hung over the field of battle, and cast gloom upon the whole region for many miles around. And sometimes the very heavens seem to veil their glories, lest they should mock individual grief. So at least it appears to the sorrower. The last two days have indeed been dark and dreary; but they have brought relief; inasmuch as dead certainty is more endurable than dread suspense. The worst is over. We bow to the decree, and yield to the absolute necessity of continuing our travels.

Under ordinary circumstances, this city furnishes the traveler with many interesting objects for contemplation. Its historical associations are not few in number. The house is standing in which the author of Faust was born; and we were told it was the place whence the world-famous Jew family—the Rothschilds—originated. We have had but a glimpse of the city, and have seen only a few of its principal buildings. This morning we uncovered our heads in the cathedral wherein the emperors of Germany were crowned for many years. The *Kaisersall* where we saw likenesses from Conrad I. to Francis II., we next visited; and afterward a gallery of statuary, where we saw the exquisite piece of private property, " Ariadne and the Lion." Driving through the Ross Market, we saw the fine monuments of Goethe and Guttenberg, both of which are admirable works of art; and the latter we thought should have a statue erected to his memory in every land, and in every city of importance in the world. Leaving the heart of the city, we rode round its edge, where the residences of the wealthy citizens stand. They presented a most attractive appearance, many of them fronting upon the fine public walks and gardens which encircle this city.

August 5th—The Rhine!—After breakfast, without the slightest wish to remain an hour longer within the city of Frankfort, we packed our portmanteaus and prepared to depart. The leaden clouds still overshadowed us, and threatened rain, when we got into the railway carriage for a short ride to Mayence, whence we embarked on one of the very narrow iron steamers to descend the Rhine. Scarcely had the passengers taken their seats, when the rain began to fall, and the wind to blow it upon the deck. The slight awning, which was hardly more than a protection from the sun, proved an insufficient shelter from the storm; and those who had taken an outside seat in order the better to see and enjoy the scenery, were soon obliged to change places. Almost all day the rain continued to fall, and the weather was depressing and tempestuous. It bore some resemblance to the grief and agitation of the feelings of our own minds. Nevertheless, neither the darkness of day, nor the heavy weight upon our spirits, had power to prevent us from looking, and

becoming interested and excited as we looked, upon the
" *Panorama du Rhin !*" Not to speak of the wondrous scenery piled up before our vision, nor of the eager interest which
seemed to animate all our fellow-voyagers, the mere
thought that we were actually floating upon the bosom of
a river which history and poetry has rendered so renowned, was alone calculated to stimulate our minds.
We were at once in the midst of stirring associations, and
were carried back to by gone ages, when travelling on the
Rhine was not so safe and pleasant—though far more adventurous—than it now is. Then, the voyager knew not
whether he should ever get beyond the next turn in the
stream; or, if he did, whether the passage would not cost
him the loss of all that he possessed. Then, the towering
mountain-tops were crowned with uninjured castles, standing in all their grim strength and terror, and their lordly inhabitants preparing, perchance, to bring death and destruction
upon some unsuspecting, though not unenvied baron.
Then horrors were perpetrated upon noble and innocent
men, to satisfy the fiendish passions of their captors—acts
of cruelty far more terrible than death. Now all is
changed, and we say " A blessing on the Rhine !" Ah !
the dead past was indeed a dread past, and a Christian
man must rejoice more in the "living present." Truly as
the centre of one of those dark, damp, horrid corridors, ex-
cavated in the very heart of the mountains, was the darkest, so were the middle ages the darkest of all, and witnessed the most unrelenting tyranny and blood-thirstiness
that the world has ever known. Luther was the deliverer
not of his own country alone, but of the world ; and never,
unless the Bible shall again become chained, will the
terrors of the past be reproduced.

But romance. as well as history, and fancy as well as
fact, has woven a net-work of enchantment over this region. Bingen, on the one hand, recalls the story of the
mouse-tower, and the vines of ancient growth which
cover the mountain-sides recall to our mind the poetry of
" vine-clad hills." The beautiful wooded islands which
we are constantly passing, the precipices of sheer rock
rising far above our heads on either side, and the crumbling ruins which, more than all else, invest the Rhine with
undying interest, combine to fill the mind of the spectator with emotions too varied and tumultuous to be with
ease described.

We envied the hour spent in the tiny cabin whence we
could obtain only a port-hole view (*less* than a " bird's-eye"
view) of the impressive panorama. But the excitement of
mind and exposure we had undergone rendered it necessary that we should take some bodily stimulant as well;
and so, following some fifty or more passengers into a
little apartment, which would not, under other than ex-
traordinary circumstances, have been judged of sufficient
size to accommodate one-half of that number, we took
seats at what might, by a great stretch of courtesy, (though
not an arm's length in width,) be called a table. But it
was made to hold a great deal. It would be a difficult
matter even to conjecture from whence came the bountiful
supply of eatables. The ship must have had an India-
rubber compartment. Course after course was put upon
the " shelf" at which we sat; and notwithstanding the
time occupied in making occasional excursions to the
deck, (that all the passing sights might not be lost,) none
went away unsatisfied. Hunger on board the little river
craft, and at its miniature *table d' hôte*, was evidently un-

known; nor could one complain of thirst after having drunk a bottle of the famous Johannisberg wine.

The after-dinner event of the day was the passing of the castle of Rolandsack, and of the forest-embowered convent of Nonnenworth, on an island in the river directly opposite the ruined castle. The mournful story of despairing love, as told by Schiller, will never be forgotten while language remains, and even now brings tears to the eyes of those whose feelings are not easily stirred. More than the superstition of Andernach, and the countless other legends of the Rhine that rivet the attention of the listener, does this tale of patient misery affect the heart—not in the way of weak sentimentalism, but with those more noble impulses and thoughts which filled the mind of the hero of " Hyperion "—the desire to live; to carry on the grand campaign of life; to wage war against evil, and overcome with good!

At length the shadows of evening fell; the rain ceased; and the sky was all of a mellow, golden hue. Not a few with whom we had commenced the journey were no longer with us. All was quiet. Silently we glided through the water. It was a time of peace and content. We thought of those who had journeyed with us down the river of life for years—who had looked forward to the time when they should be so situated as we then were, and likewise look upon these hills crowned with hoary castles, or covered with cheerful clusters of grapes, and enjoy all the pleasures incident to the tour. But they had gone where pleasures are forevermore, and left us behind. In the full flush of their young life they had passed away. "Death," says the author of the "Lady of the Lake," " is dreadful at all ages; but in the first springtide of youth, with all the feelings of enjoyment afloat, and eager for gratification, to be snatched forcibly from the banquet to which the individual has but just sat down, is peculiarly appalling." And so it would *seem;* but may it not be that they had already enjoyed the banquet—those whom we counted lost? We had been enjoying the " Paradise of Germany ;" but were not they enjoying the Paradise above ?

August 7th.—For years we had looked upon the Cathedral of Cologne, (or Cöln as it is called here) as represented in very accurate engravings, and wondered whether we should ever stand within its walls. For years we had been familiar with the mysterious legend relating to the architect of the magnificent edifice, and conjectured as to whether we would be permitted to behold its unfinished tower. To day we have done both! one is oppressed with its immensity when viewed without, and contrasted with the highest buildings standing beside it ; and impressed with its vast and magnificent proportions as, with bare head, and light tread, he reverently enters, and stands transfixed with mute admiration. Truly it is the grandest work that man's hands have ever yet formed. One feels when viewing it, that undefined, undefinable awe which moves one when witnessing some great phenomena of nature. Worship becomes instinct in such a place; and it needs not the voice's of the priests, nor the transporting music of the choir, to lead one to do homage to man's creator.

Besides this first and awful building. we have seen other famous edifices for which Cologne is celebrated ; but there are others which we have not visited, although well worthy of being inspected even at great sacrifice. Among these is the house in which the immortal [painter. Rubens. was born; and several venerable churches of note. But we have seen enough to employ our tongues, and occupy our minds! and this afternoon we 'are off for Brussels; the "little Paris" of Belgium.

August 8th, Brussels.—As we sit by our windows in the Hotel de Belle Vue, and look upon the fine statue of Godfrey of Bouillon, in the handsome square of the Place Royal, we are forced to concede to the universal opinion that the Belgian Capital is a delightful city. With the gaity of Paris it appears to possess something of the solidity of an English city, and it has many worthy claims upon the time and attention of the visitor. The Palace of the Prince of Orange; the Hotel de Ville; the Cathedral; the church of St. Jaques; the Museum and "Musee de la Industrie" and the Lace manufactories are some of the most interesting objects to be seen. The beautiful spire of the Hotel de Ville, (Town Hall) was something to which our notice was especially called; and it is indeed worth studying. The hall itself was undergoing repairs; but we were so fortunate as to gain admittance, and were conducted by a guide through the handsome senate chamber and hall of representatives. The former presented the appearance of a theatre far more than it did a place for political discussion. All its appointments were tasteful and elegant. Before leaving the hall we were shown portraits of the King * and Queen, and a piece of tapistry very remarkable on account of its great age. But some of the choicest pictures, by celebrated artists, which we saw in the mu-

---

* *Since deceased.*

scum afforded more entertainment than aught else. One by
Reubens, particularly. The coloring of the flesh and gar-
ments, considering their great age, is really wonderful.
Not being distracted by the multitude of paintings which
bewilders one in the galleries of Paris, we studied them
quietly and more deliberately, and thought them exceedingly beautiful. What a privilege do they enjoy who can
come daily and drink in the full expression and deep meaning of these masterly works of art ! A long drive in and
about the city, has enabled us to appreciate its spacious
Boulevards, gardens and fine monuments, which make
Brussels so bright and cheerful and add so largely to the
happiness of its inhabitants.

August 9th, Waterloo.—Having secured a private conveyance last evening, we left the " Belle Vue " about ten
this morning for the field of Waterloo. After a pleasant
ride of two hours, the greater part of which was through a
cool, shady wood of spruce and pine trees—the forest of
Soignies—we arrived in the village about two. Picking
up a guide at the little hotel near the village, we drove
around the field, and were made acquainted with the various locations of the armies and their commanders. It is
said that the guides have three separate stories of the battle. One for the English, another for the French visitor,
and a third for the American traveler. But however this
may be, our guide seemed to be possessed of some accurate information, and was " born upon the spot." Our
first visit was to the farm of Hougoument, where the
English were concentrated in force. Here we put our fingers
into the bullet-holes in some of the old walls still standing, and picked some little blue-bells from the spot where

the fight had been the most determined, and where the grass
grew as if it still luxuriated from the blood which had there
been shed so lavishly.   Next we ascended to the top of the
" mound" monument, erected in the year 1852, and took
a general survey of the celebrated battle-field.   The
guide continued to point out the place where this or that
attack was made, and the precise spot where this or that
general was killed.   It was a place to learn great lessons
—the folly of human greatness and godless ambition.
Here the man who had defied the world—the great though
not the good man—was crushed, humiliated, defeated.
The man of blood, who used human life as a tool to exe-
cute his schemes of self-exaltation, met with a just retri-
bution, and saw his armies—even that division under his most trusted and greatest general, Marshal Ney—
defeated, cut to pieces, and almost annihilated.   What
Napoleon's feelings must have been when his last well-
disciplined corps was repulsed, and when there were no
reserve regiments at hand to whom he could issue the stern
command, " Onward ! Onward !" no ordinary man can even
imagine.   We could well nigh weep for him, so intense must
his sufferings have been.   Defeat to his finely-organized,
proud spirit, must have been many times worse than death.
In an hour his career of success and glory was at an end, and
he was reckoned among the great but unfortunate heroes
of the world.   So long as the sun and moon endure will
men continue to hold various and antagonistic opinions
regarding his character—to bless or to curse his memory.
But so long as the world endures must the author of the
" *Code Napoleon*" be had in lasting remembrance.   Until
the time shall come when " nations shall learn war no
more," will men be found who will delight to honor the

mighty general, to hang *immortelles* upon his monument, and make a pilgrimage to the spot where his remains are entombed. The intellectual, too, will worship his wonderful powers of mind; and, above all his countrymen, " the French people," will constitute him their patron *saint*, point with pride and delight to those grand and beautiful edifices which adorn their capital, and exalt him as the greatest of the great—the incomparable *Empereur*, Napoleon Bonaparte.

We returned by the ordinary road, passing the little inn in which the Duke of Wellington lodged. We stopped at a small church, where many of the officers and privates who fell upon the hotly-contested field hard-by were either buried or had tablets erected to their memories. Several of the inscriptions were affecting, and most all interesting, on account of the youth of the victims. We reached the hotel about half-past six, and after some refreshment rambled through one of the principal shop-streets, visiting the well-stocked galleries of Goupiel & Co., (with its familiarly sounding name,) the handsome arcade of St. Hubert, and several smaller establishments. Stopping at one of the latter—a glove emporium—one of our party purchased a pair of gloves; but for some reason or other did not succeed in getting them on with ease. Fearing they were too small, or would not bear the strain put upon them, he made some remark to that effect; whereupon, much to his surprise, the young girl reached over the counter, took possession of his hand, and with a few vigorous pulls—such as no inferior article could have endured composedly—proved the correctness of her judg-ment by making the article fit exquisitely. The thing was done in a trice, and in a perfectly dignified man-

ner; and although there was, perhaps, the slightest
possible expression of displeasure on the good-looking
face of the girl, she manifested it in no other way; and no
extra charge was made on account of the unusual honor
conferred.

August 10*th—Antwerp.*—Visited this old city to-day.
It is as dull at the present time as it once was prosperous.
But it will always attract the traveller while those grand
old temples and works of unrivalled art remain within its
ancient walls. We have, to-day, stood upon the pavement of its famous cathedral, and viewed those wonderful
paintings by Rubens, the descent from and the elevation
of the cross—pictures the like of which we had never seen
before, and which, having been seen once, are never to be
forgotten. They are not to be *looked at* merely, but to be
quietly, earnestly studied. Paint is the most insignificant
part of these masterpieces—the necessary material only—
the coloring, notwithstanding the age is wonderful; but
it is the *expression* of the whole and of each part that
makes the works so glorious. Truly Rubens must have
believed in his heart that the scene which he has so represented as to enrapture thousands was really enacted;
and may it not be considered as a proof of the divinity of
the subject of both paintings, that these great productions
of a marvelous genius possess the power to rivet the attention of the beholder, and so affect his heart? May it
not be that many a man has gone from the presence of
these eloquent though silent preachers of Christianity, to
examine the foundations of that system which he had before that hour regarded as a weak superstition? While
we would hope that such good results have been accomplished, it cannot be doubted that, aside from the deep

pleasure and satisfaction they have yielded to hundreds of
adoring pilgrims, their presence in the city is, like the art
treasures of the Italian cities, a means of support to not a
few of the inhabitants who gain their livelihood by exhibiting them, and by satisfying the wants of the many
travelers hitherward.

The church itself, with its cloud-touching and very
beautiful spire, is an interesting object to contemplate
and admire, as are several other structures which we afterward visited. Indeed Antwerp is rich in splendid church
edifices, as well as in their valuable adornments. The
museum, also, contained many productions of art, deserving more than the few moments that we could spare for
each of them. Paintings by Rubens, Van Dyke, and
others. Two pictures—the decapitation of John the Bap-
tist, and the martyrdom of a certain saint—were among
the most horrible that had ever met our vision.

After dinner, at the fine Hotel St. Antoine, (during the
preparation of which we read with regret of the failure of
the second attempt to lay the Atlantic cable,) we climbed
to the top of the tower of the cathedral, whence we obtained a superb view. We looked into a new country, one
we had not seen, and did not intend to explore. To the
east, the monotonous plains and canals of Holland were
plainly visible. From thence came Rip Van Winkle, his
successors and predecessors. It would have been interesting, in some respects, to have visited the Nether-
lands; but we had not yet seen our own fatherland; and
so, with one wistful, lingering look, we quitted the cathedral. Driving through the commercial part of the city,
we passed the fine dock built by direction of Napoleon,
and, in the course of our drive, saw the handsome steam-

yacht in which Queen Victoria had come from England to attend the inauguration of the monument erected to the memory of Prince Albert, at Saxe Coburg Gotha. The *quays* are evidences of the importance of Antwerp as a great sea port, at one time; and even now the neighboring region is the livliest in the city.

August 11th—Brussels to Paris.—Left Brussels at an early hour, in order to accomplish the long journey of 215 miles before night. We met with little incident during the ride; and before six o'clock were again in Paris, and among the favored guests of the magnificent Grand Hotel. It is very pleasant to be in this sparkling city again. It seems for the moment like being at home. Notwithstanding all the delights experienced during our three weeks' tour in Switzerland, Germany and Begium, it is a satisfaction to be where one can hear regularly from loved ones at home. The thrilling enjoyments of the past are over, it is true, and may not be enjoyed again save in the revelings of memory; but what *has been* is ours; it cannot be forgotten; and were our pleasures to end here, we should have thoughts laid up for many years, and be grateful for the inestimable privileges and opportunities we have enjoyed of seeing with our eyes some of the greatest wonders of the world.

August 15th, Paris.—It is evening, and the great *fete* day, called the Emperor's, is ended. It has been a great day to the children of the Empire, and a very novel one to the stranger within the gates of the imperial city. Leaving the hotel about two, we drove as near as possible to the *Plaza des Invalides*, where the multitude were

7

chiefly assembled to witness the free theatrical performances, gymnastic exhibitions, tight-rope dancing, etc., etc.
The first of these amusements was highly sensational, and
even the occasional very tragical death of some one of the
performers partook largely of the ludicrous (although
very popular with a majority of the spectators). Not so
the feats of strength, some of which were astonishing;
and it was wonderful to note the perseverance with which
(allowing themselves but brief intervals of rest) these sons
of Hercules continued to excite the applause of the pleased
spectators. It seemed, too, as if the poor dancing girls
would utterly fail; but still they kept it up, round after
round, without any flagging. Perhaps the most amusing
of all the " sights" was the climbing of the greased poles.
One adventurer would go but a little way, and give up
the undertaking; another, when almost to the top, and
within but a short distance of the prize, would (either
for want of strength or patience) come down amid the
groans of the multitude; while a third, carefully hus-
banding his strength, would finally succeed in reaching
the silver regions, and after picking a flower, and making
a hasty choice, would seize a silver tankard, and, while
cheer after cheer rent the air, quietly slide to the ground.
Occasionally a *furor* would be caused by some wild re-
port that the Emperor (who was known to have lately
repaired to the camp at Chalons) was coming, and the
excited crowd would look in every direction in which it
would be possible for his majesty to approach. It did not
take many moments, however, for them to become again
absorbed in the surrounding pleasures of the hour. About
three, the rain began to fall, and for a time the crowd
scattered. Now the venders of wine and divers sorts of

refreshments became very busy. People of all sorts, seeking shelter from the rain, filled their tents or booths; and as all who availed themselves of these coverings were expected to spend a few *sous*, the owners reaped a good harvest. Soon, however, the people became accustomed to the rain; and as there was no cessation of the free performances, they again filled the open spaces, and all went on as before. Mingling with them freely, to see for ourselves, and enjoy their enjoyment, we were astonished at the good humor and total absence of all roughness.

Each and every one seemed to be quietly pursuing his pleasure, and what if many of the pastimes seemed fit only to beguile a child, so long as they answered the purpose of bringing joy to the hearts of the common people, whose daily toil was constantly adding to the beauty of the city, and increasing its innumerable attractions. How can men who have scarcely sufficient leisure to obtain necessary sleep and recreation be expected to be more than children in intellect. And certainly a better behaved multitude were not to be found in any part of the world. None were noisy; not one did we see who was in the slightest degree intoxicated. Besides the greater attractions prepared for the amusement of the people by the government, there were a legion of lesser centres of attraction gotten up for the purpose of private speculation, by people who were willing to forego the listless enjoyment of the day themselves, if by any means they might add to their precious store of savings by amusing their fellow-countrymen, and thereby secure a small portion of the *sous* which would be spent to-day by the poorest peasant.

From the time the rain commenced, it continued with
brief intermissions until past seven o'clock. About
half-past five, we left the scenes of festivity, and drove to
the Restaurant de Petit Moulin Rouge, in the *Champ de
Elysee,* where, with keen appetites, we enjoyed a well-
served and in all respects most satisfactory dinner. Dinner over, we again took seats in the carriage, and went to
see the fireworks. But all the avenues leading to the *Champ
de Mars* were guarded, and it was impossible to approach
the spot whither the whole city (save the poor soldiers
who had been confined all day in the barracks) were bend-
ing their steps. But at length we succeeded in getting
upon a somewhat elevated road, and here we waited
patiently until the hour when the display was to take
place should arrive. It was some time before the signal
rocket was fired, and the air was raw and damp. But
when at length the magnificent display commenced, we
forgot the past in the surprise and delight which the entertainment afforded. The "bouquet," as the last piece
was called, was beautiful beyond description. It was
soon over, and we were following in the wake of a line
of carriages a mile long, and driving through all the illuminated parts of the city on which vehicles were allowed
to enter. For the first time in many years the occupants
of the carriages were allowed the privilege of a short
drive in the *Champs de Elysee* on the evening of this August day. The place looked transformed, and with the
brilliantly lighted *cafes* and resorts of various kinds on
either side of the broad avenue, it presented a truly dazzling appearance. In some of the Boulevards through
which we rode were buildings, the windows of which were
glittering with light; and the various devices and inscrip-

tions in honor of the Emperor, and in commemoration of
the day, were striking and beautiful. Altogether the
illumination, though not as brilliant as might have been
expected, was enlivening, and could not well have been
spared from the generous entertainment. The reaction
would have been too great had the gorgeous blaze of fireworks, when they died out, left the city in gloom. It was
more fitting that the joyous excitement should gradually
subside, and light after light should go out, as score after
score of the people went to their homes. And so it was.
And when, near midnight, we entered the illuminated
court of the hotel, we did not regret that the end had
come, and that we had witnessed the successful termina-
tion of the great " *Empereur's Fete*."

August 23d.:—The end of our second month of travel
finds us in Paris, and better acquainted, at least with its
outside life, than during so brief a residence amid its splen-
dors, we should have supposed possible, and than would
perhaps, have been possible had we not enjoyed the guid-
ance and companionship of our esteemed friends Dr. and
Mrs. James B. Gould, of Rome, (formerly of New-York,)
whose long residence abroad has made them well acquainted with Paris, as well as Italy ; and who have, fortunately, apartments in the Grand Hotel.

The Parisians walk about, and in all respects act, as if
hurry and worry were to be avoided as much as the
plague, and we found that by imitating them we really
learned more of Paris life, than we would or could have
done had we maintained those restless, anxious habits
which characterize so many of our countrymen. For a
couple of *sous* one can secure a seat in the lively square of

the *Palais Royal*, and by sitting there, and opening his
eyes and ears, he can learn and see more in a single afternoon, than he could in several days spent in many other
determinate though ill-directed endeavors to become acquainted with the people and their customs. We had been
dining at the Cafès, attending the open air concerts in the
Champ de Elysee; continuing our evening rambles through
the arcades and passages, varied by an occasional attendance
upon some place of amusement; visiting the mint and other
places of interest not before visited, doing a little shopping, and so forth. To our regret we have not yet seen
the Emperor, although we visited some days ago the
Palace of the Tuilleries. Although the Emperor is absent, evidences of his power and authority are not want-
ing. The work of the embellishment of the city still goes
on. A great deal of destruction is preceding the *recon*-
struction; but it may perhaps be doubted whether the
Emperor is not a demolisher of men as well as of build
ings. He is crafty, and knows too much thought
among the people is not good for them; or, if good for
them, is not likely to strengthen the hands of an absolute
monarchy. Every exertion is made to gratify sense, and
special efforts are put forth on Sunday to induce the
people to regard it as a gala day; to cause them, as one
well expressed it, to "forget that they are accountable
beings." Still, one may live as he pleases in Paris; and
this is the special privilege of all who reside in large
towns; although few cities command the advantages
which one who resides in Paris may enjoy. Few others
offer the same opportunities for high mental and scientific
culture, and not one holds out so many attractions to the
mere votary of pleasure; and although religion appears

to be as little thought of as a poor man, yet it is a mis-
take to suppose that one cannot be religious because he
is in the midst of a gay throng, of whom it may be truly
said, that "God is not in all their thoughts." In most
things it may be best, "when in Rome, to do as the
Romans do;" but it is not always essential, nor is it
always right.

Thursday, August 24th.—It is seven weeks this morning since we landed at Havre. To-day is to be our last
in Paris and on the continent of the Old World, as we are
hoping to leave for England—upon the soil of which land
we have not yet trodden—to-morrow morning. We have
taken a long stroll on the Boulevards, Rue Rivoli, Vivi-
enne, St. Honoré, and other of the livliest streets, taking
a parting look at the shops, and purchasing a few last
mementoes of our visit. Have this evening looked for
the last time upon the gay gas-lit streets, swarming with
inhabitants of all ages and characters, and which are for
brilliancy unequalled in the world. Taken our first and
last dinner at the *table d'hote* in the magnificent *Salle a
Manger* of the hotel, and are now about to lie down and
seek a final night's rest beneath a veritable "French
roof."

Friday, August 25th—France to England.—Breakfasted
a little before eight in the restaurant of the Grand Hotel,
and not long after, for the fifty-first and last time, drove
out of the grand court for the handsome depot of the
"*Chemin de fer du Nord.*" At nine o'clock and ten
minutes, precisely, the train left the depot, and at half
past one reached Bologne. Here we were detained an

hour, being conveyed to the pier in omnibuses, and being obliged to wait the arrival and shipment of the baggage. The crossing of the channel was accomplished in a couple of hours, and with but slight discomforture to a few of the lady passengers only. We were especially fortunate, not only on account of the weather, but because of our meeting with valued friends, whom it had been our happiness to greet both in Geneva and Paris. The fresh breeze and salt air were very refreshing, and many concomitant circumstances tended to raise our health and spirits. On our arrival at Folkestone, we landed amidst a concourse of people. We felt that we were indeed " a sight to behold," being not only weary and travel-worn, but travel-soiled as well. However, we were not disposed to quarrel with the fair Saxon girls who had come to welcome us to the shores of " Merrie England."

By the express train we were transported, in less than two hours, to Charing Cross Station, and descending, like St. Nicholas, from the region of chimney-tops and of smoke, with our packs upon (not our own, but the porter's) backs we were, in less than ten hours from the time we left the French capital, in London ! The examination of our luggage (no one travels with *baggage* in this country) was very slight, but one trunk and one bag, out of the three trunks and three bags, being opened. With no very long delay, we were rattling over the pavements in the direction of the Palace Hotel, Buckingham Gate, where we found quiet, comfortable, delightful quarters. After getting rid of the dust of travel, we dined; and during the evening B. and myself walked down the Strand in search of a map of London. This morning we ate breakfast in Paris—this evening we were strolling in

London! It is pleasant to hear our own tongue spoken by all around us again, and to be able to get what we want without *fear* (there was no ground for fear, as the French never laugh at others) of making people laugh at us because of our trembling, hesitating pronunciation of the French. So much real, earnest life do we expect to find here, which one might look for in vain in Paris, that it is a relief to feel that the transformation has taken place.

Saturday, August 26th.—The change from Paris to the equally-famous, though more solemn, city of London, is great. It was hard to realize, on waking this morning, that we were really in the mother country—in the land whence came those from whom we were lineally descended, and where those great men lived and labored whose immortal works had helped to form our characters and inform our minds. Whatever may be the feelings which one nation may bear or may have born towards another, justice demands that prejudice should not be allowed to interfere with the appreciation of intrinsic worth. So long as reverence and affection are stronger than hate, so long must all true-born, noble-hearted Americans love old England. Though the younger nation be equal in power in many respects, and superior in natural and undeveloped resources to the elder, yet how can she speak with hatred of that land from whence the pilgrim fathers came! (*Vide* Macaulay.) The land from which she derived her language, and, indirectly, her solid character and consequent strength. We have no affection for titles, no slavish cringing before the British Lion, and yet we rejoice that we are in England.

We left the hotel about half-past twelve, and drove first to the office of the old American banker, George Peabody, where we obtained letters from home. The names of the streets through which we passed were very familiar—the Strand, Cheapside, Haymarket, Fleet, Ludgate Hill, etc. We passed the huge and grand edifice of St.—Paul's "Old St. Paul's"—the theatre of thrilling scenes so intimately associated with the history of the city, and many monuments erected to the memory of famous Englishmen. Our first "sight" was, justly, that of the Tower of London! a relic of the time of Julius Cæsar, if not of some earlier monarch. We saw the water-gates through which Queen Elizabeth was wont to pass on her way to Westminster, the White Tower, Beauchamp Tower, chapel, jewels, etc. Walked round the entire pile, and spent in all some two hours in and about the momentously interesting spot. Laid our throat upon the beheading block, the same (we were told) from which the head of Anne Boleyn fell. Saw the executioner's mask and axe, and some instruments of torture used by the Spanish inquisition. Went into the room or cell where Sir Walter Raleigh spent thirteen years of his life in close confinement, being employed meanwhile upon his history of England. The underground dungeons were closed. In the Beauchamp Tower we spent some time deciphering the inscriptions; among others were these, "*Sic vive vt vicris,*" (so live that thou mayst live,) "*Et morire ne moriericris,* (and die that thou mayst die not). The name was T. Salmon, and there was a crest formed of three salmons. The device and mottoes we are not likely to forget. Another, "Hope to the end, and have patience," seemed especially appropriate to the place. "Patience!"

was apt to work out "experience" here; and it seems to have had that effect upon this word sculptor, judging from the weighty and wise sentiments he has elsewhere inscribed upon the walls of the cell. Many incidents connected with these carvings are truly affecting as well as interesting. Many an inscription here would, we think, furnish an excellent text for a sermon; as the lives of some of the personages whose names are here recorded have yielded the materials for more than one fascinating work of fiction.

While passing through the White Tower, the warden called our attention to the skillful arrangement of various parts of different weapons which (formed into ingeniously contrived devices) adorned the ceilings of the apartments. One in particular represented the " Passion Flower." He also directed our attention to the " Harmour of Enry the Haighth," and to the thickness of the walls; in some portions measuring fourteen feet! Having stood for a moment in the chapel, and listened to the history attached to it, as narrated by our courteous conductor, we descended to the court, and entered the Jewel House. Here, beside the crown jewels we saw the precious fount from which the water was taken wherewith the Prince of Wales was baptized; his crown; etc.

Leaving the place, around which so many powerful associations cluster, where kings once dwelt, and illustrious men and women were sheltered or murdered, we drove to the Thames' Tunnel, representations of which had adorned our geographies from our earliest no-nothing days, and excited our infant wonder. And truly it is a wonderful work! Whatever else may be said about it, one thing is certain, and that is, that although it may *go down*, it can never *burn down.* For the amount of one penny we were permitted to descend to the region of perpetual night and dampness, and, after walking through its entire length, we ascended to the street on the opposite side of the river. During our passage forth and back, we were besought to purchase various articles offered for sale by the occupants of the stalls; but the constitution both of the goods and the venders of the same, had become affected by the humidity incident to their location, and neither presented a very attractive appearance. It is a singular place to spend one's days in, descending at sunrise and ascending at sunset. Shut out from all the world, these denizens of the Thames seem not to apprehend that the explosion of the powder magazine of some ship might shiver their alabaster cups into a thousand pieces, and destroy not only their business but their lives. It is not probable that the explosion of the *boiler* of some one of the river steamers over their heads would cause them the slightest discomposure. Fortunately, their thoughts do not soar so high; and the only matter for regret is, that, notwithstanding many of them attain a good old age, these honest, contented, happy people, do not live out half their *days.*

August 27th, Sunday.—This morning we went to Westminster Abbey, consecrated not only as a place for worshiping God, but also as a monument in which to immortalize man. Still, it may justly be observed that the works of most of the men to whose memory tablets have here been erected, do glorify God, and their authors are, therefore, appropriately remembered within these venerable and sacred walls Cannon Hawkins

(Aukins, we were informed) preached a good sermon from the text, " Canst thou by searching find out God?" The grand old Abbey seemed an appropriate place in which to argue so great a question—a question which every thoughtful man has, at one time or another, sought to solve, and a vital question in a land where the great responsibility of life is acknowledged, and the Sabbath at least outwardly observed. Whether all could say " Amen !" at the close of the discourse, God only knows. The preacher's answer to the problem was, that " Man did not find God ; but God came to and found out him."

In the afternoon we attended St. Paul's. Owing to the respect shown for religion in this city, and to prevent the worshipers from being disturbed, vehicles are obliged to stop at some distance from the entrance, and the occupants to walk quietly to the door of the porch. Entering, with others, within the vast building, we were in a moment standing beneath its lofty dome, and receiving the impression with which the vast proportions of the architecture of the interior of this magnificent edifice inspires one. With a feeling of awe we followed those who had preceded us into one of the chapels, and heard a most beautiful choral service, and a discourse of a profitable kind. It was late when the service closed, and we had little time to notice the marble monuments, but expect to go again for that purpose very soon.

August 28*th*.—This morning we went again to Westminster Abbey. Our party was increased by the society of Mrs. H., and together we looked at the monuments, and read the inscriptions, erected to the memory of the princes and poets of Great Britain. Saw tablets erected to the memory of Shakspeare, Milton, Spenser, Chaucer, and others too numerous to mention, in the Poet's Corner; and in the chapels, including Henry the Seventh's, through which we were afterward shown, the tombs of Elizabeth, her unhappy sister Mary, Charles II., William and Mary, etc. As we reverently trod the sacred aisles, we felt, as Washington Irving, in his most feeling and truthful "sketch" of this famed abbey has so well expressed it, "as if we were disturbing the hallowed silence of the tomb," and that we were "surrounded by the congregated bones of the great men of past time, who had filled history with their deeds and the world with their renown."

Next we visited the magnificent Houses of Parliament. Although at first refused admittance beyond the passages leading *to* the House of Lords, on the one hand, and of Commons, on the other, we at length, by patience and perseverance, succeeded in obtaining a view of these richly ornamented houses, and also of the picture gallery, robing room, and libraries. After viewing for some time the fine picture of Moses, with the stone tables containing the ten commandments, we drove to the British Museum, and there passed the remainder of the day. Saw a manuscript of one of Shakspeare's plays; also, handwritings of Scott, Macaulay, Washington, and others; many curious and ancient volumes; the Egyptian Antiquities; and so much that was deeply interesting that we were very loth to come away. To most visitors the splendid library is more attractive than the mummies and the lamps of the ancients. We certainly preferred to look upon the stereotyped brains, the most *substantial* remains of great authors, rather than to inspect the

" heads of collossal dimensions" of the ancient Egyptians. We copied but a single line which accompanied an engraving of Shakspeare, and was as follows :

> " This figure that thou here seest put
> It was for gentle Shakespeare cut,
> Wherein the Graver had a strife
> With nature, to out-do the life.
> O could he but have drawn he his wit
> As well in brasse, as he hath hit
> His face ; The print would then surpass
> All that was ever writ in brasse ;
> But since he cannot, Reader looke
> Not on his picture, but his Booke."

Tuesday, August 29.—Greenwich.—Went by boat upon the Thames to Greenwich, and visited the handsome old hospital, where the veterans of the navy find a home, after their age and infirmities disqualify them for further active service. A sail through this famous river, in the very midst of the densely populated city, offers one a good view of the tower, the London docks, and other objects of interest. Among others, the ship yard, where the greatest of ships, the Great Eastern, was built. There are innumerable landings, and the river seemed as greatly crowded with crafts of all descriptions as are the streets with all sorts of vehicles. We were astonished with the rapidity and skill with which these hundreds of little iron steamers were piloted under the arches of the magnificent bridges, and through narrow passages, seemingly impassable. Steaming over the heads of the living inhabitants of the catacomb-like tunnel, we were soon alongside the " Dreadnaught," and immediately thereafter landed at Greenwich dock, whence we had a fine view of the commanding pile, which seems to stand as if hewn out of solid rock ; and, as a home for those who have spent their lives upon the ocean, presents a strong contrast to the ever-restless, turbulent sea, upon which they have spent so great a portion of their lives. After looking at the portraits of various commanders, and representations of stirring naval engagements in the Painted Hall, and the various relics of Nelson and the Franklin Expedition in the Upper Hall, we went into the chapel, where we saw West's Shipwreck of St. Paul. Passing out upon the broad stone piazza, we saw the blind, the halt and the lame sailors ; some of them stooping from age, walking, sitting and talking ; and heard them testify to the comfort in which they lived. Most of them sat facing the observatory, from which they had so often reckoned "Longitude west from Greenwich ;" and the Hospital seems in all respects an appropriat place for them to rest in at last. As we were passing from the hall of one of the buildings, an old sailor approached, having a stick in one hand, with which he seemed to be feeling his way. Mrs. B. asked him if he were blind, " Yes," he said. " But your eyes look bright," she responded. " Yes, Ma'am," he answered, " too bright," "too bright." We went away reflecting on his words, and thinking how applicable they were to the *seemingly* bright lives of many a weary, world-sick soul.

August 30*th.*—Went first to Madam Tussard's Exhibition of Wax Figures, The models were surprisingly natural and life-like. One in particular, representing an old woman, leaning upon her stick, and viewing the collection, we mistook for a being of flesh and blood. Another, an old Quaker gentleman, with the usual broad-brimed hat upon his head, and placed upon one of the seats, intended for visitors, was so inimitably represented that visitors in

variably stepped out of the line of his vision. Almost the
first figure that met our eye was the manly presence
commanding form, and mild, though decisive countenance,
of George Washington! It was, indeed, a "speaking
likeness." Groups of the Royal Families, and principal
personages of France and England: Luther, Rosseau,
Penn, Shakspeare; actors, heroes, poets, statesmen, church-
men, Kings, Queens Presidents, divines, murderers, con-
querors, and the great ones of all lands were wonderfully
represented. Now and then it would strike the beholder
that these notabilities were living beings. Lincoln and
Davis were represented as talking amicably together, as if
attempting to adjust the affairs of the nation; while, in an
adjacent room (especially appropriated to statues of murderers) Booth, the assassin of President Lincoln, might be
seen. Booth's statue had been advertised as one of the
greatest recent acquisitions of this class. There were
also to be seen relics of Wellington and Napoleon, and
the costly coronation robes of George IV.

Nest we went, to the Royal Mews, or stables, where we
saw the handsome horses belonging to the Queen, and the
state and plain carriages of H. R. H. Queen Victoria.

Last of all we drove to the National Academy, and remained about two hours. Some two or three paintings
might justly have occupied the time devoted to the entire
collection. A few by the great masters, some of Rubens'
domestic scenes, were the choicest. Turner's productions
occupying one entire gallery, require much study, in order
to be appreciated. So, at least, we judged. An evening
drive in the Strand and elsewhere, in order to see something of "London by gaslight," finished the "order of

exercises" for the day, and gave us enough to think and to dream about for more than a day.

August 30th.—To Sydenham.—It does *not* rain as (we were told it did in this country) all the time. The sun shone brightly and hotly enough on the occasion of our first ride about the city, to give one of our party a hard headache; and it has shown most of the time, as if to contradict the unfavorable impression we had formed, that we should experience nothing but gloomy weather, and English dislik to United Statesmen, or as everyone calls our counytrmen here, *Americans.* Relying upon the promise of continued dry weather, we took an early start for Sydenham, in an open carriage. Driving down Victoria Road, through Belgrave Place, etc., we crossed Chelsea Bridge, and passing Battersea Park, were soon in the suburbs of the city. The sun being partially obscured, and the weather not oppresively warm, the ride was a very pleasant one, and yielded us the opportunity of seeing some of the beautiful suburban cottage residences. Nearly all of them had names printed on the gate or boundary posts, and many of them were very pretty, as Ivy Lodge, Effray Lodge, etc. Arrived at the Palace, we drove under the covered portico, and passing the recording gate, entered the wondrous fabric of glass and iron. A mere sight of the light and beautiful structure would have afforded an ample compensation for the journey. It seemed as if it were indeed a castle built in the air; but one, underneath which a substantial foundation had been placed. The fruit exhibition, which was the special display at this time, was the finest in some respects that ever we had looked upon. The grapes were unequalled; the size and

beauty of the clusters rivalling any we had ever seen
before. Passing through the various courts, we found
much to admire; interesting specimens of antique architecture, of different lands and ages, and many beautiful
pieces of statuary. Among the latter there was a
plaster cast, the subject of which was a warrior's wife,
mourning over her husband who had fallen in battle, and
embracing the noble animal upon which he had ridden
to the fatal field. The intense and hopeless sorrow depicted in the mourner's face was truly affecting. Many
other works of art attracted our attention, and are worthy
of the praise bestowed upon them. The foreign and
tropical plants located in the naves of the palace were
curious and beautiful, and the green of the higher trees
contrasted with the crystal walls inclosing them, formed
a picture very agreeable to the eye. We also saw the
bark of the " Wellingtonia Giganta ;" the California tree,
supposed to be 4,000 years old, and it is consequently
probably the oldest thing contained within the transparent
walls of this elegant edifice. While going the rounds of
the galleries we occasionally caught sight of the tastefully
arranged terraces, walks, statues, and fountains of the
handsome grounds surrounding the Palace ; but, although
we spent a number of hours within the glittering structure,
we found no time to visit them. During our tour through
the arcades, we were reminded of the booths of Baden
Baden, so multitudinous was the variety of fancy goods
offered for sale within the place. Indeed, we found as
much entertainment in gathering souvenirs of our visit in
those lively little shops, and in the galleries of the palace,
as we had done in viewing many of the lesser attractions
of the place. It happened quite accidentally that we

visited the Crystal Palace on a "shilling day," as it is called; and consequently the class of people whom we met, were the very class who enter most heartily and simply into the pleasures of the hour. Who come in the morning and remain until nightfall; and to whom the varied enjoyments of the day, inclusive of the grand concert, is a season of "unadulterated happiness." Our own pleasure was increased by the sight of their happy faces, and the interest and intelligence which they displayed. We left them in the very midst of their enjoyment; but it was pleasant to think, as we drove away from the exceedingly grand and magnificent palace, that there were hearts within its walls whose joy was as pure and light as the crystal roof above their heads. This evening we have been to a concert at Covent Garden, where we heard Charlotte Patti sing, and some wonderfully fine clarionet music. There were few occupants for first class seats and boxes; the first families being either at their estates or at Brighton or elsewhere; but there came up a volley of uprorious applause from the parquet, which was crowded to excess, both by occupants of the seats, and those who had procured promenade tickets. There were some four or five different prices of admission. The performance was, upon the whole, a very enjoyable one; notwithstanding the house was neither "brilliant" nor "fashionable."

September 1st.—The summer (so far as its *name* is concerned) is over and gone. But there is nothing in this bright and beautiful morning betokening the incoming of the delightful, "sweet, melancholy days" of autumn. Going into the reading-room, before breakfast, to look at the *London Times*, we had the pleasure of shaking hands with Cyrus W. Field, who is a guest in this house. He seemed in no wise discouraged at the second failure of the Atlantic telegraph, and said they "had only come back to get a little more ammunition."

Strolling through the "Bird Cage Walk," we took one of the little steamers from Westminster Bridge to London Bridge Pier, and thus went "down town." We visited the Royal Exchange, Bank of England, Browne, Shipley & Co's., and a number of the shops; and were finally driven rapidly home in one of the "hansomes." Although we had seen hundreds of these vehicles flying through the city, we had not entered one before, and were highly pleased with our experience of them; they were navigated through the crowded streets as skillfully and as rapidly as the iron steamers of the Thames are piloted through the numerous shipping of that river. Notwithstanding the length of the reins, the jehu seemed to have perfect control of the animal. When we had occasion to speak to the driver, a trap-door in the roof formed a convenient medium of communication. We have been struck while riding about the city, with the peculiar effect which the weather and climate produce upon the buildings; making the new ones look like old ones, and the older ones to appear as if built of different kinds of stone; and giving a look of great antiquity to the edifices of the great metropolis. So much is there to be seen and quietly enjoyed in London, that some are tempted to think seriously of taking up their permanent abode within sound of the Westminster bells. There is a wonderful combination of art as well as nature within the limits of the city. A drive of a few minutes, or a walk of not immoderate length will conduct one from the bustle of the city into the quiet and rural

seclusion of Hyde Park, or into the midst of the fine collection of plants and animals in the Botanical and Zoological Gardens of Regents Park. Here one may receive
much instruction, as well as entertainment. Many parts
of London—Trafalgar Square, for instance, presents an
appearance of strength and nobleness unequalled by portions of any other cities in the world.

Sunday, September 3d.—London.—Went this morning to
the Scotch Free Church, Crown Court, Covent Garden.
While waiting for the pew holders to take their seats, had the
pleasure of meeting with James M. Brown and family. As
we were not allowed to enter until just before the service
commenced, we had the pleasure of inquiring after mutual
acquaintances at home. And when at length we were permitted to enter the hallowed, though very plain chapel, it
was a privilege to worship with those whom we had known
in our own homes across the sea ; with them to pray and
give thanks unto Him who doeth all things well. We
listened to a very simple, thoughtful discourse from Dr.
Cummings. He had nothing to say about the " Great
Tribulation" this morning. Perhaps he holds not the same
views he once held upon that subject, at the present time.
From the very mild manner he exhibited while deliver-
ing the very thoughtful discourse, one might imagine that
he had himself become a child of the Kingdom, "through
much tribulation." Afternoon went to Surry Chapel,
where Rowland Hill preached for fifty years ; but we did
not hear Dr. Newman Hall, as he was absent from the city.

Monday, September 4th.—Left London in the noon train
for Windsor Castle, the residence of the noble Queen of

England. First of all, on arriving within the enclosure
of the grand old palace, we climbed the Keep or Round
Tower, whence we obtained a fine view of the beautiful
surrounding country. It is said that a view of twelve
counties can be had from the height. Next, we visited
St. Joseph's Chapel, where Edward IV., who commenced
the building, is buried. Here we saw the exceedingly
beautiful and mournful cenotaph erected to the memory
of the Princess Charlotte, and a monument of more recent
date, placed here by Queen Victoria, in memory of her
mother. The sculpture upon the face of it represented
the lady's acts of Christian benevolence—feeding the
hungry, clothing the naked, visiting the imprisoned, and
ministering to the afflicted. We also paused to notice
the new altar piece erected by the Queen to Prince Albert's
memory, etc. As the Royal Family were expected to return to Windsor during the day, we were disappointed in
not being able to gain access to the state apartments ; but
after visiting the Riding House, enjoyed a drive in the
"Long Walk," two-thirds of the distance to Snow Hill,
upon the crown of which we saw in the distance, the
statue of George III. Having time to visit neither Frog-
more nor the Virginia Water we drove to Eaton High
School or College, and visited its library, and dining-room,
etc. Upon the walls hung portraits of those who were
"foundation scholars" within these old walls at one time;
but who had achieved name or fame in their land, and
whom the college now delighted to honor.

September 7th—London.—Yesterday we made a long
and special visit to St. Paul's Cathedral, the greatest
building in Great Britain, and in size among the largest in

the world. We first examined the fine statues to the heroes of the army and navy, and then visited the whispering gallery, library, clock, and bells; and thence climbed to the ball. Having climbed into the ball for a moment, we descended to the platform surrounding the Golden Gallery, from whence a most extended view of the vast and seemingly limitless city, is obtained—a city containing buildings a thousand years old!—a city whose power had been felt throughout the world; and yet it was made up of individual men and their works alone. Hundreds of men whose deeds have immortalized them, and some of whose forms, sculptured in marble, surround the inner walls of this wonderful temple, have walked in the shadow of the cathedral, and are no more; and still the busy conflict of life goes on, and the interest in things present swallows up the interest in things past, and, in too many instances, the interest in the things to come. The " golden" gallery is indeed a rich spot whence to garner a harvest of thoughts; but a man must take a comprehensive view with his mind's eye, as well as his natural eye, if he would preserve his reason, unless (as did the artist who once spent several weeks in the dome while engaged in sketching the wonderful prospect) he intends to take up his abode in these sky regions. Fortunately we were obliged to descend. To-day we have taken a last look at old London Bridge; a last sail on the Thames; a final drive beside the Serpentine in Hyde Park; a farewell stroll through Regent Street; and having given directions regarding our letters, intend leaving London on the morrow.

Friday, September 8th.—By a singular combination of

unforeseen circumstances, the weekly return of this day
has almost invariably found us journeying somewhere.
Not only did we set sail from our native city on Friday,
but on the third Friday we journeyed to Rouen, on the
fourth to Geneva, on the fifth to Lucern, (and a memorable journey it was,) on the seventh from Brussels to Paris,
and on the eighth from Paris to London ; and *this* morning we took an early start for Scotland. Leaving our
very pleasant home-like quarters in the Palace Hotel.
about nine o'clock we reached the handsome station of
the London and Northwestern Railway in good time ;
and having taken seats in the " through " carriage for
Edinburgh, were soon out of the city, and enjoying some
of the beautiful meadow scenery of England. We left
London with regret, notwithstanding the fog, and the
smoke, and the mud, of which Frenchmen visiting the
country complain so bitterly (and we know that some
Frenchmen think as much of their polished boots as we
do of their polished manners). We have not been in any
wise inconvenienced by either of those elements. The
earth has been dry, the air fine, the fire (smoke) has remained in its appropriate regions, and the water (rain)
has not in a single instance, during our stay in the city,
descended upon our heads. Upon the early morning
one day only was there any fog. Whatever may be
the predominating climate of the land, we believe the
moral atmosphere is constantly improving ; that there is
enough of the leaven of goodness and the principle of
growth, physical, intellectual, and religious, to preserve
it from destruction ; and not only to preserve it, but to
promote the increase of the powerful influences which
go forth from this great centre into all the world. Eng-

land and America—that is, the true and noble men and
women in both countries—are pledged to the same work;
to uphold and extend the same privileges and blessings
into and throughout all the regions of the world. Would
to God that there were more such women as Queen Victoria, and such men as our immortal Washington, in these
present days, and every land were blessed with the life
and labors of a St. Paul.

We had none but pleasant recollections of our visit as we
journeyed northward. At twelve, we arrived at far-famed
Rugby, where "Tom Brown" spent his happy school
days. At Preston, which town we reached about half-
past three, we lunched, and about six arrived at Carlisle.
Soon after leaving the latter place, we crossed the little
river, and were in Scotland. The sun, which had shown
upon us every day since our arrival, in Great Britain, (a remarkable fact, if the stories of previous travellers are to be
credited,) illuminated the fields, and made the water of the
streams to sparkle during most of the way; and we had dust
in abundance. It was between nine and ten o'clock when
our long day's journey came to an end. Tired and hungry, we sought the Royal Hotel, but could gain no admittance, and were recommended to the tender mercies of a
Frenchman named Dejay, the keeper of the Hotel Fran-
cais, where we found English comfort and French fare;
and after recruiting on *poulet* and *cognac*, wooed "tired
nature's sweet restorer."

September 9th.—Edinburgh.—As we sit at our window
to write the record of this day, there looms up before us
the wonderful old Castle of Edinburgh, built upon the
rocks. Never, should our lives be spared, ("e'en down to

old age") shall we forget our visit to this ancient castle
and fortress, within the walls of which we have this
day spent several hours. The view of the city; the surrounding country;—including the Salisbury Crags and
Pentland Hills—together with the Frith of Forth;—as
seen from the plateau, upon which stands Elizabeth's little
chapel, (also discernable from the windows of Dejay's,) is
altogether one of the most impressive we have yet seen.
We could have passed days upon the battlements, viewing the wide and fascinating landscape. It stirred up the
depths of our minds, and revived tender associations of
years gone by. There is a mysterious sympathy between
the body and the mind—between bodily heights and mental heights. The little chapel, Queen Mary's crown,
sceptre, and sword of state, as well as her private apartments in the tower, were all visited. Reluctantly we
left the castle, and drove to the interesting palace of
Hollyrood, where we were shown the identical bed in
which the unfortunate Queen of Scots once slept, the
room in which Rizzio was murdered, the blood stain upon
the floor, the picture gallery, and so forth. We trod
reverently the pavement of the crumbling abbey, and lost
the opportunity of being immortalized in connection therewith by not remaining within the sacred enclosure while
an artist took a photographic view of the ruins. Strange
things happen in these latter days, when people can sit
quietly in their parlors at home, and yet see the mountains, and castles, and old abbeys of far-distant lands;
and there is something singular in the thought that these
haunts of history are being represented upon pictured
cards, to be transmitted to all parts of the world, by an
art which was (when these old castles stood in all their

glory) undiscovered and undreamed of! In the very
room in which stood the veritable bed upon which Queen
Mary reposed, we bought card photographs representing
that room and its contents, perfectly, even to the tapistry
hangings upon the wall, and the hole in the door opening
into the secret passage—by means of which Darnley and
his confederates succeeded in effecting an entrance into
the supping-room adjoining, and enacting the fearful
tragedy in the very presence of the Queen. And so it
was, go where we might, an opportunity was afforded us,
of carrying away not only an image of the interesting objects in the mind's eye, but accurate representations of
those objects upon which others as well as ourselves
might look, and from the view receive pleasure and instruction.

Leaving the deeply interesting edifice of Holyrood, we
enjoyed greatly a ride in the Queen's Drive, almost entirely surrounding the Sailsbury Crags, from whence we
obtained new, beautiful, and extensive views of the neighboring country. In the course of our ride, as we passed
St. Anthony's Well, children came running after the
carriage, and offering us glasses of water from that crystal
spring, or pebbles from its stony bottom. Further on
we came in sight of the cottage (or the place where the
cottage once stood) in which the heroic Jennie Deans
once abode, and from which she set forth, in God's
strength, upon her long and perilous journey of love and
mercy. It was very pleasant riding thus amid the classic
localities of " Mid-Lothian," which *the Scott* of Scotland
—and of all the world thus far—has rendered famous.
The hour was toward sunset, and the shadows were
lengthening all about us, while the emerald green of

Arthur's seat was bathed in light. There was indeed much enjoyment afforded us in that ride of one short hour. We would have prolonged it indefinitely had it been possible.

Sunday, September 10*th, Edinburgh.*—This is a great city in which to hear sermons. Preaching is not confined to the churches, which are numerous; but if one is not too tired to stand, he may listen to extemporaneous discourses delivered at the corners of the streets with unsurpassed earnestness and solemnity. The Sabbath question is much agitated, and the running of Sunday trains uncompromisingly condemned. All the inhabitants of the city appear to be church-goers, and happiness, content and health appear in the faces of those whom we meet in the street. We have ourselves heard two very excellent and orthodox discourses. The first, preached by Dr. Alexander, of the Independent Church, was a fair sample of the style of that eloquent divine. The text chosen was the sixth verse of the sixth chapter of Ephesians, ' As the servants of Christ, doing the will of God from the heart." " Words," said the speaker, " orginally addressed to the slave," but which might be construed in a broader sense to apply to all God's children upon earth. We might view God's afflictive providences submissively, and this was well; but the perfect and highest attainment was to view them as manifestations of God's character, as not not only good, but the best. An earthly sovereign might give laws not in accordance with his real character; but the providences of God were not only discoveries of Himself, but a very part of Himself. We should believe that God wills what befalls us, and that therefore it is best." Such were some of the comforting and assuring

words which fell upon our ears, and were treasured up
in our hearts; and although the manner of the preacher
was cold, we could not but believe that his sympathies
were warm.

Afternoon, went to St. John's Episcopal chapel. As
the service had commenced, the doors were not only
closed, but locked; and we were about to leave, when
the sexton opened a very small door on the east side of
the church, and we were invited to enter. The edifice,
within and without, was a handsome one; and although
the dimness of the religious light, and the height of the
pew enclosures, made it difficult to see either preacher or
people, it did not prevent—nay, it aided—our enjoyment
of the beautiful and not unprofitable discourse upon the
scripture promise, "Thy peace shall flow like a river."
The preacher spoke of looking from nature up to nature's
God. He dwelt particularly upon the illustration in the
text; spoke of the purity of the stream compared with
the men who dwelt upon its banks, and whose strifes
and passions caused so much misery. The beginning of
the river, like the budding of grace in the soul, was
sometimes almost imperceptible. But it grew broader
and deeper as it advanced, until, at last, like time, it
reached the ocean of eternity. What could man do without the river of life? What if men were not prepared
to enter upon the ocean of eternity!

Monday, September 11th.—*Edinburgh.*—Our visit to the
celebrated University of Edinbro', this morning, was
one of more than ordinary interest, from the fact, that
some whom we had known had been educated within its
walls. Here more than one great man had in his youth

garnered rich stores of the very highest classic and scientific knowledge, and the erudition, both of those who have been students, as well as those who have been and are professors in this college, has caused it to be celebrated as one of the first and highest institutions of learning in the world. We were shown into the spacious library, the floor of which was carpeted, and the room wore a delightful air of comfort and seclusion. It seemed a fit storehouse for the works of those writers whose thoughts have, to a great extent, " ruled the world," and an appropriate and pleasant place in which to study the productions of those masterminds. In short, it was just such a place as a study should be. The museum was undergoing alterations, and a cloud of lime-dust prevented us from extending our observations in this direction. After visiting the Royal College of Surgery, where we found much to excite our interest and curiosity, as well as our wonder and admiration, and enough to occupy more time than we had at our command, we drove through Nicolson Square, and George's Square, (on the west side of the latter, once stood the house of Walter Scott's father,) and arrived in due time at Hariot's Hospital, a most noble institution, for promoting the education of the sons of reduced citizens, and which has for more than two centuries been in successful operation. Passing through the chapel, dormitories, assembly room, and so forth, we learned much regarding the studies, character and manner of life of those who had been and were the privileged inmates of this school, and saw a likeness of George Hariot, the distinguished founder ; and also portraits of some of those who had made themselves names in the world, since leaving this, their early home. In passing through the court, we noticed that many of the small, square stones with which it is paved were numbered; and upon inquiring into the cause, were told, that each boy, upon his first enrolment as a member of the school, received a number by which he was afterward designated and that whenever the school was called together—previously to marching to chapel or elsewhere,— each pupil was required to stand upon the particular pavement bearing his number. By this simple contrivance, it is said, much confusion is avoided and better discipline secured. The vacation had just expired, and we saw some of the well-dressed smaller boys drawn up in line just as we were leaving the grounds.

Next, we visited the Botanical Gardens. After enjoying a ramble through the greater portion of the fine grounds, and viewing the choice and curious plants with which they are enriched, we visited the extensive greenhouses. While within these glass structures, we climbed the spiral staircase leading to the galleries in the upper portion of the building; but found ourselves not only amongst the tops of the tropical palms, but in the midst of a tropical heat so intense, that the perspiration poured from every pore of our bodies, as if we were undergoing a Russian vapor bath. Leaving the garden, we changed our position, and stood upon Carlton Hill, whence a good view of the city is obtained, and upon which stand Nelson's, the unfinished National, and Playfair's monuments, and also the Observatory. After some time spent in enjoying the varied and fine prospect, we descended the steps fronting the debtor's prison, and driving to the National Gallery, visited its collection. We closed this well-spent day (during the course of which we have, perhaps, seen more than in any one day since we landed upon the shores of the old world,) by a visit to Greyfriars, the scene of the sufferings of so many holy men, who died martyrs to the faith : Who died like their Saviour, that others might live through their triumphant testimony.

September 12th.—Occupied the day in journeying to the little village of L., in Fifeshire. We had a somewhat misty sail across the Firth of Forth, in the steamer " Forth," and reached our destination about noon. Here, though not far distant from Edinburgh, we were in the midst of the quiet and seclusion of the country, and, much to our satisfaction, learned something of the peasant life of the Scottish people. Entering one of the houses of the cotters, we were particularly struck with the neatness and comfort of their abodes; and the books upon the shelves betokened their appreciation of the advantages of an educated mind. Some of them, though humble, and contented with their sphere of life, are yet acquainted with other than their native tongue ; and even the young women, in one or two instances, were good Latin and French scholars. Through the influence of Christianity alone have the common people of Scotland become even more elevated and refined than the same classes in England ; and far more so than the peasantry of any other European country. Religion leads them to respect and cultivate themselves, and raises them in the social scale ; and what else could or would accomplish this end ? Would that those who possess greater privileges and knowledge of the world had more of the power of religion in them—that we had, during the past years of our lives, " *done,* instead of *doubted*—warred, instead of wept."

There is, perhaps, something more impressive in a jour-

11

ney into the quiet, solitary, rural districts of a foreign
land than there is in a visit to its great cities; inasmuch
as there is more change in the latter. But when one
contemplates the hills and valleys across which generation
after generation have wandered, or the village green upon
which the children of each succeeding generation, for a
thousand years, have sported, and which have always
been the same; he begins to experience a feeling of awe
weighing down his spirits, making it impossible for him
to give utterance to the thoughts that fill his mind.

September 13th—*Edinburgh.*—The experience of every
hour in this grand and delightful city is so fraught with
interest and pleasure, that each day deserves a separate
record. About twelve, went into the Antiquarian Museum
of Scotland, and spent more than an hour in examining
the various relics of past ages therein collected. Some of
them were Grecian, some Egyptian, and others Indian;
but the more part, and the most interesting portion, con-
sisted of sculptured stones and coins, which had been dug
from the very soil of Scotland; proving its great age as
an inhabited and civilized country. Afterward we drove
to Leith, and walked to the end of one of the very long
piers, extending almost a mile into the water. Although
it is only the middle of September, the wind was blowing
with such force from the west as to make the undertaking
well nigh dangerous and difficult of accomplishment. Returning to the city, we visited the house in which John
Knox lived, and from a window of which he delivered
his sermons. We sat in his study chair, read a psalm in
his Bible, and passed through, one after another, the deserted rooms. Being the only visitors, we had a good

opportunity to inspect at leisure aught that attracted
our attention. But it is not always pleasant to visit even
the haunts of those who have long been dead, when the
noise of one's own footsteps in the deserted chambers is
the only sound that is heard.

September 14*th—Edinburgh.*—Driving to the Scott
monument this morning, B. and myself ascended to the
top of this magnificent structure, and enjoyed the fine
prospect for about half an hour. This splendid testimonial
is worthy the city and the man. Its history is most interesting; and the only sad circumstance connected
therewith is, that the talented architect was drowned before the edifice was finished. Having from this height
viewed, for the last time, the scenes of the birth-place of
those events of which all the world has heard, (and will
continue to hear,) through the genius and labors of the
man to whose enduring memory this monument has been
erected, we drove to Roslyn Castle and Chapel, distant
six miles from Edinburgh The excursion occupied the
remainder of the day, but well repays one for the time
and strength expended in making it. The chapel is a
most beautiful and interesting specimen of architecture,
equaling in those respects, though small as to size, any that
we have seen during our travels, and is many hundred years
old. It is indeed a rare gem, and we spent a long time in
studying and admiring its special beauties, sculptures, and
inscriptions. The story of the wreathed pillar, and of the
founder, and the noble hound who saved his master's life,
interested the visitors much. The guide also explained
at length the meaning of various portions of the adornments of the chapel. The ruins of the castle situated in

the midst of most enchanting scenery, were next inspected, and afforded us an example of the strength, gloominess, and, to a certain extent, *wierdness* of the castles of the olden time. On our way back to the carriage—after a walk, through a part of what was, at one time, a portion of the magnificent terraced gardens of the palace—we stepped for a few moments into an old burying-ground not far-distant. We found, among others, one old tombstone, containing the following quaint lines :

> " Underneath this sod doth lie
> As much virtue as could die,
> Which when alive did vigor give
> To as much virtue as could live."

We left the spot about three, and returned to the hotel in good time, much delighted with the day's experience, and with appetites that did ample justice to the turtle soup, and all the other good things which had been carefully prepared with special reference to our farewell dinner in " Old Reekie."

Friday, September 15th—Edinburgh—Glasgow.—The fated day (Friday) having arrived, we propose journeying to Glasgow this afternoon, and this morning have been to see the handsome Register Office, and St. Giles' old church, at the latter place Knox preached, James IV. made a farewell address to his subjects, and a certain Dean's head came into contact with a vulgar stool. The old women who were engaged in cleaning the different chapels were at first apparently much annoyed at our in-trusion; but after a time became very communicative, and at length we were obliged to tear ourselves away from their highly interesting society before the half had been told us. Although their appearance was not pre-possessing, their conversation evinced that they were by no means ignorant of the historical associations connected with the floors which they scrubbed. One story in particular engaged our attention. It was in relation to the old custom of bringing condemned criminals to church (and to this venerable edifice in particular) upon the Sabbath previous to their execution; and the manner in which, upon a certain occasion, one of two miserable men brought hither enabled the second and younger to escape, not only from the custody of the soldiers, but from death—he himself, the deliverer, losing his own chance of escape that the other might live. Leaving this interesting place, we went to the Gallery of Statuary, containing, it is said, one of the finest collections of plaster casts in the United Kingdom, and including, among others, the Apollo Belvidere and Dying Gladiator.

Evening.—Arrived in Glasgow per the Edinburgh, and Glasgow R. R., about four o'clock. Not knowing that the Queen's Hotel was just thirty steps from the station, we waited some moments, in order to secure a conveyance, and were at considerable labor to bestow ourselves within and our effects upon the top of the carriage, and had only just established ourselves comfortably for the ride, when, to our amusement, the coachman having turned the corner, informed us that our journey was ended. After a quiet, pleasant dinner in our rooms at six o'clock, we went to Argyle street—the Broadway of Glasgow—to walk, and strolled up and down for about an hour, looking in occasionally at a shop window, and doing a little shopping. Our first impressions of Glasgow are, that though a great, and a busy metropolis, it is still a somewhat dull city. Full of churches, and containing many bad characters. But this latter characteristic is perhaps not to be wondered at, considering the vastness of its manufactures, and the great number of those employed therein.

Saturday, September 16th.—Went this morning to visit the Cathedral, once and for a long time the place of Roman Catholic worship, but now called the High Church, and no longer filled with the incense of superstition, or the mummeries of the priests. Although not comparing in grandeur with many others which we have seen, the edifice abounds in legendary and historical associations. The traditions concerning St. Mungo, the reputed founder, appear too wonderful and contradictory to be true, especially the miracles he is said to have wrought. "It is affirmed, that after he came to years of understanding, he did never eat flesh, nor taste wine or any strong drink ; and when he went to rest, slept on the cold ground, having a stone for his pillow ; and that, notwithstanding he lived thus hardly, he did attain to the age of *ninescore* (!) and five years." But although the age of the founder may well be discredited, there can be no doubt as to the antiquity of the church itself; and it was a singular fact, that some of the stone found upon the ground, which had become embedded in the soil with which the building was repaired some years since, bore marks, proving it to be a portion of some earlier temple of worship which had been erected on the same spot. Scott, in " Rob Roy," does well to call it " A brave kirk ; a' solid, weel-jointed mason wark, that will stand as lang as the world,—keep hands and gunpowther aff it." But had it not been for the Government mandate, at the time of the Reformation, the frenzied people would, in their endeavours to " purge it of all kynd of monuments of idolatrye," and make it " a mair Christian-like kirk," have destroyed it altogether. The mandate was as follows : " Fail not, bot ze take guid heyd that neither the dasks, windocks, ner durris *be ony ways hurt or broken*, either glassin work or iron work." The structure was subsequently arranged to accommodate three distinct congregations. The oak pulpit in the inner high is many times older than the oldest preacher that ever occupied it ; being, it is supposed, 700 years old. Passing through the beautiful Lady Chapel, we next descended to the Crypts, originally intended as the burying place for the priests ; but subsequently used as a place of worship. The " dim, religious light" was very dim indeed ; and it is to be hoped that the spiritual illumination which came to those who here, in very truth, " sat in darkness and in the shadow of death" exceeded the material light by which they were surrounded. Having previously examined the handsome painted windows, the subjects of which are almost wholly scriptural, and the number of which is very great—furnishing, as it were, a lithographed Bible, which all may read and understand—we bestowed a few moments upon the various monuments and inscriptions. Many famous men have walked these floors. Bruce and Cromwell have been within its walls ; but no creature of royal blood who has ever visited the Cathedral is more worthy of fame and admiration than Queen Victoria, who, some fifteen years ago, came hither for the purpose of view-ing its beauties. Before getting into the carriage we visited the church-yard, where the slabs are arranged in rows upon the surface of the ground, and so closely

that almost every foot of the enclosure, save the few
narrow paths intersecting the tombstones, is covered.
It solemnizes one's mind, this peculiar arrangement,
but does not strike one at all pleasantly. It seems
as though these heavy weights had been placed upon
the breasts of those who were asleep in death to prevent
them from coming forth out of their graves. No
" living green" is seen, for there is no room for it to
grow ; and all seems as cold and stony as death itself.

Next we went to the College of Glasgow, bearing
the date "Anno Dom. 1654,'" upon its exterior. This
old building, together with the Cathedral, are the most
interesting specimens of the antiquated architecture of
the city. Driving to the Green, and from thence along
the river side to Glasgow Bridge, and beyond, we returned by the way of West End Park, where the new
and handsome residences of the wealthier portion of the
community are located, and the new free church College
stands. We saw the spot whereon the old University
is to be newly located, on the opposite side of the Kel-
vin, and many of the principal streets of the city. Evening, walked in Argyle and other streets. The whole
city—that is, the humbler classes—seemed to be out of
doors, and by far the greater portion of them appeared
to be quite young. No doubt they belong to the number
of those who are daily confined to hard work in the
numerous manufactories of the city, and whose whole
life is one long continued struggle for existence.

Sunday, September 17*th—Glasgow.*—About ten, we
ascended the " Bell of the Brae," as the higher part of
High Street is called, to hear Rev. Dr. Norman Macleod ;

but were disappointed in not hearing him. However, we listened to an excellent discourse from the nephew of the illustrious clergyman; and although he was quite a young man, we thought the Doctor could not have had a better substitute. For the first time, we noticed the posting of a large card near the pulpit, prior to each singing, designating the tune to which the hymn or psalm was to be sung. The large church was well filled, and the assembly seemed really to enjoy the service, so heartily did they join in it. After dining at the *table d'hote*, at 5 P. M., by request, (instead of in our own rooms as usual, in order, as was stated, that the servants might be permitted to attend church—another proof of the Sabbath-keeping character of the Scottish people.) we went into a neighboring place of worship, where we heard a very earnest, stirring, impressive sermon, from Acts: "And as he reasoned of righteousness, temperance, and judgment to come, Felix trembled, and said, when I have a convenient season I will call for thee." Seldom, if ever, have we listened to a preacher with more attention, and such a sermon it would perhaps be impossible for one to hear out of Scotland. The speaker divided his discourse into three heads: 1st, the model preacher, Paul; 2d, the convicted hearer; and 3d, the dangerous procrastination. Paul, he said, spoke with great fearlessness and boldness to Felix, who was a cruel, licentious, worldly man; rebuking his vices; preaching to him right government, temperance, and judgment to come; and Felix so far forgot himself and his position—he was so moved by the the Spirit of God—that he *trembled*. (Had any present trembled?) But he gathered up his skirts and passed out of the room, sealing his destiny by his choice and his

fatal delay. Would any before him defer that day? The
preacher spoke as one who felt that much depended upon
his preaching—upon the words he uttered at the moment—and so warm were his appeals to those present
that it seemed strange to see the people quietly sitting in
their seats. To one unaccustomed to such an impassioned
style, it would seem as though the very walls must cry
out.

Monday, September 18*th—The Clyde.*—Left in the
eleven o'clock boat, starting from Glasgow Bridge, and
sailed down the Clyde as far as Greenock. Saw the
large ship-building yards, where the wonderful vessels of
the Cunard and other lines (by means of which thousands
annually cross the ocean) are constructed. Passed Dum-
barton Rock, famed in history as the place of the confinement of Wallace, and as the foundation of the castle
which was taken by Crawford in so bold and remarkable
a manner. We looked upon it with great interest before
reaching it, and long after we had passed it, remembering
the while the admiration and fascination with which,
during the years of boyhood, the reading of the "Scottish
Chiefs" had inspired us for the character of Wallace.
Some of the views were charming; and the sky being
overcast, the sail was very enjoyable. But one incident
occurred which was not in all respects pleasurable.
When about half way between the G's, (Glasgow and
Greenock,) not the boat, but a passenger upon the boat,
took fire. The conflagration was caused by a spark from
the smoke-stack of the steamer, and in a few moments
smoke was seen to issue from the folds of a rich and becoming silk basque upon the person of Madame ——. As-

sistance was immediately rendered, but not until the flames had extended; and so far as the appearance of the article was concerned, it was totally destroyed. Fortunately the lady sustained no irreparable loss—her insurance being ample—and she took no other notice of the occurrance than to change her seat, lest, should another firy shower descend upon the deck, her person as well as her wardrobe might be consumed.

Arrived at the seaport of Greenock, we walked up into the town; and after refreshing ourselves at a place where there were so many eatables of a palatable description that we did not know which to choose, we employed a driver and carriage, in order to see all that was worth seeing. These objects were not a few, besides the beautiful drive by the Firth, and a fine view of the entire town, river and mountains from the Whin-hill. Returned by rail to Glasgow about five o'clock.

*Wednesday, September 20th.—Ayr.—*Yesterday we passed a quiet day; and having seen our friends off for Ayrshire, (they have gone in search of a portion of their past lives,) we went into the Royal Exchange to read the *London Times* of yesterday, and a file of the *New York Times* for the past month. During all our travels we have not seen a finer edifice consecrated to the divinity " News." The latest intelligence from all parts of the universe is posted upon bulletins at the upper end of the handsome hall as soon as received, and one need not be at the trifling labor of looking for it in the papers, although many duplicate copies of all the most important sheets in the world, including " The New York World," abound " The stranger, as well as he that is born in the land," has the privilege of frequenting this truly *Royal* Exchange at will. Sauntering through the beautiful Argyle Arcade, one is much interested in noticing the beauty and great variety of the Clan Tartan, (Scotchwood,) articles exposed for sale. Besides the hundred and one specimens of these goods which have already been carried across the water, and which we had seen at home, we found many new and choice paterns of exquisite workmanship. We were told that the inventor had accumulated a large fortune, and that most of the articles were still printed at one particular place.

This morning left Glasgow in the half-past ten train; reached Ayre about half-past twelve o'clock. The ride along the coast was very pleasant, and some of the views were charming. Arrived at the pretty gothic railway station, we paused a moment to admire its very ornamental architecture, and then passed up the principal street in search of the "King's Arms Hotel." A single direction from one of the "honest men" was sufficient, and we reached its sheltering arms just in time to be protected from the descending rain. Taking possession of the sitting-room, which was fortunately a front one, and on a level with the street, we found entertainment in reading the "Scotsman" (advertisements and all) and one of Sir Walter Scott's novels, and in looking at the outside world. At times it rained hard; but the bonnetless and "bonny lasses" who passed the widow seemed as much accustomed to water as they were to Ayr, and, by their very laughter, shook the rain from off their nutbrown cheeks and tresses. The town is more than usually lively, in anticipation of to-morrow's races, and the annual county ball of Ayrshire, which it is anticipated will bring to the town greater numbers than are at present gathered here. Booths have been erected in some of the principal streets, and the people are rejoicing in prospect of the temporary excitement. About five, went to meet the friends who had preceded us, and conducted them to the hospitable King's Arms, where we soon after dined. The " King," we were informed, could entertain us but one night, as the apartments assigned us had been engaged for some time past by those who intend to thread the mazes of the dance to-morrow night. But we were well content, as we had no intention of remaining to witness the Ayr ball, and we certainly did not care for the *foot ball* part of it. Evening, went out to visit the " Twa Brigs." We crossed the auld one, and recrossed the Ayr River by the new. The only " dialogue " we heard was carried on by ourselves, in reference to the structures but no doubt, had we remained long enough, the Brigs might have told us many a tale of by-gone years—in imagination, at least.

September 21*st*—*Ayr.*—We drove this morning first to the cottage in which Burns was born; and after walking through it, and inspecting the likeness with which the inner hall is adorned, purchased a view of the building itself, and next visited Alloway Kirk, where Tam O'Shanter saw the witches dance. Thirdly, we visited the Burns Monument—a fine commemorative work. Its site is well chosen, and the view from the top is a very lovely as well as grand, embracing ocean, mountain, plain, as well as the romantic grounds surrounding the monument itself, together with the birth-place of the poet, the Old Kirk, and Brig O'Doon. In the lower portion of the edi-

fice, within the small square room, we saw some mementoes of Burns, and of his Highland Mary. After sauntering through the grounds, comparing our watches with
the sun dial, and remembering our guide, (in considera-
tion of which he allowed us to pluck a bit of mistletoe as
a souvenir of our visit,) we got into the carriage, and after
riding a short distance, got out again, and walked over
the bridge spanning the Doon. Here we listened to the
de-tailed account of Tam O'Shanter's passage of the Brig,
and of his narrow escape from the witches. Driving
thence to the little inn, we went for a moment into the
small shell grotto, an ingeniously arranged little cabin on
the banks of the Doon, and after looking upon the humorous
statues of auld Tam O'Shanter and Souter Johnny, his
boon companion, we took *our* glass of ale, and departed.

Afterward drove to the race course, and attended the
Western Meeting, where, taking our place in the line,
we passed the remainder of the day. Saw some of the
fashionables of Scotland, who came in their handsome
elevated equipages, and, with few exceptions, remained
throughout the day. The last race took place about
five ; after which we repaired to the King's Arms, and
dined, returning to Glasgow by the seven o'clock train.

Tuesday, September 26th—Liverpool.—Adelphi Hotel.
This is to be our headquarters until we leave the shores
of the Old World. We have been in this commercial
emporium only a few days, but like it much. It resem-
bles New York in many things : in its crowd of shipping ; its street cries ; general business life, and bustle.
Our lodgings are particularly pleasant, and the quiet,
comfortable life we live within our rooms is in striking

contrast to the tumult going on without. Twice every day
our table is noiselessly and temptingly spread with luscious
food, and everything is done so quietly that it seems
sometimes as if we were enjoying the luxury of a home
in a foreign land. So well pleased are we with the
appointments of the house, that we are not sorry that
it was impossible to procure rooms in the "Queen's. On
Sunday the hush throughout the city was universal, and
we attended St. George Place chapel, where Dr. Raffles
preached for so many years. To-day we have driven past
most of the principal buildings, and visited the St. James
and Necropolis burying grounds. The former is most
singularly located, below the level of the surrounding
streets and houses; and although in the very midst of
the city, none of the thousand different sounds are heard
by the visitor walking among the grave-stones. Some of
the worthy men who passed their whole lives within the
city were here buried within its very heart; and who
could desire a higher tribute than the following, which
we found upon one of the monuments :

> " If upright worth and virtue claim a tear,
> Reader, 'tis due to him who sleepeth here—
> *Grateful, Affectionate, Sincere* and *Kind*,
> His memory's dear to those he left behind.

Though some one might wish to add to it, it is one
that the greatest and most renowned might covet. Another, a simple but melancholy one, also interested us :

> " The languishing head is at rest ;
> Its throbbings and achings are o'er ;
> The quiet, immovable breast
> Is heaved by affliction no more."

Also visited the very attractive Botanical Gardens.

where one may spend an hour most delightfully. The superior skill displayed in arranging and contrasting various plants are seen to perfection ; and particular portions of the gardens, where the flowers are planted upon terraces, are strikingly beautiful. The Wavertree Park, adjoining, we did not explore, and after a drive to Birkenhead returned to the hotel.

September 28th.—Went this morning to the Royal Gallery of Arts, where we saw some very good paintings. The best were principally scriptural subjects. Among them was a remarkably and terribly expressive face of Christ upon the cross, also " Christ disputing with the Doctors," and " Mary washing the Saviour's feet," were faithful representations. There were also casts of various pieces of celebrated statuary. The Royal Museum contains a most wonderful collection of birds and shells, and stuffed animals, made by William Roscoe. Leaving these interesting places, we went for a few moments into the Ladies' Bazaar, Queen's Hall. It was a fair held on behalf of some church, and there was the usual complement of grab-bags, worsted and other ladies' fancy work, charming girls with very winning ways and persuasive manners, and " refreshments." In short, a fair is very much the same sort of an affair the world over ; but as we fared well, and the fairs treated us fairly, we have nothing of which to complain. From this place we went to the Prince's and other docks, which extend for miles along the banks of the Mersey. It was interesting to witness the opening of the massive gates, the rapidity with which the foot-bridges are turned, and the passage of some large vessel through the dock gates. There is something curious in the perfect, immovable security (so far as the water is concerned) of a ship when resting safely in one of these artificial basins, compared with its condition when bounding upon the stormy billows of the ocean. So accustomed does one become to seeing a particular vessel in a certain given locality for many weeks, that it seems, when at length the vessel begins to move slowly and almost imperceptible toward the narrow outlet, as if a very part of the town itself was about to change its position or take its departure. It would seem as though the inhabitants must needs be a cosmopolitan people, when ships from all parts of the world, containing the luxuries and the natives of all lands, arrive daily at almost their very doors; and it is interesting for one who has no knowledge of the destination of one of these packets, to go down to the docks, and watch her progress from her secure harbor out into the sea—speculating, meanwhile, as to which quarter of the globe she is to visit; the length of time she may be absent; the strange adventures she may meet with while being borne over the vast expanse of the great deep, and the changes which may occur ere those who now set out hopefully upon a long voyage again return to their native land. Those who do business on the great waters must oftimes have thrilling thoughts and experiences. But, after all, *business* is the aim in all these transactions in commerce, though romance may be connected therewith. Of all places the harbor of Liverpool would seem the last place for a dreamer. Here all is practical, and the man of money thinks mainly of the chances and prospects of trade; of the profitable harvest he is to reap; but, after all, he is a dreamer; for is it not the dream of wealth that brings

13

him to the spot? Alas, that his anticipations should fail
of being realized. Liverpool, it is said, has doubled
itself in twenty years, owing to its vast commercial re-
lations, and is extending itself greatly in certain directions. Perhaps it would not be easy to compute the
number of dwellings erected with every new dock that
is built. "No man liveth unto himself." The *aim* of,
comparatively, a few men to enrich themselves, *ends* in
their being the means of promoting the wealth and
growth of whole cities, and of giving the means of life to
not a few of their inhabitants. The most commanding and
the handsomest building in this city is St. George's Hall.
Here we listened one evening to various performances upon
the grand organ. The selections were admirable, and so
well and feelingly executed as to bring a spontaneous
smile of pleasure upon the faces of the listeners, and
pleasant dreams to their minds. To our regret, the
affair lasted but an hour. The organist was Mr. W. T.
Best, and we thought the name a most appropriate one.
With all due respect to our countrymen, W. H. Morgan,
it was not the only Best, but *the* best performance of the
kind that has ever delighted our ears or stirred our feelings; and not knowing to what cognomens the first two
initial letters of the artist's name referred, we thought they
might not inappropriately be denominated: Wonderful—
Talented—Best.

Friday, September 29th.—Drove down London Road,
and through the beautiful private residence parks. Afterward, went into the School of the Blind, where we heard
some very good singing by the inmates. Most of them
came from their work into the small hall. There was a

rmge of sadness upon the countenances of a few, but it was mingled with an expression of contentment; and one or two faces wore the aspect of hearty good humor. The time and harmony were admirable; and we could not doubt but that their sense of hearing was much quicker, and their enjoyment of the music much greater, than it would have been had they been in the possession of all their faculties. The small audience room was full to excess, and the sympathy awakened by the earnestness with which the singing and chanting was executed, and the misfortune of the singers, made the occasion a most interesting and affecting one. The pieces were mostly of a religious composition. We afterward saw the blind men making baskets; and, going into the wareroom, looked at the great variety of wicker and worsted work, and other articles of various descriptions. After purchasing some mementoes, we left the place much pleased with our visit. Reached the hotel about four; and just as we were entering, we were reminded that our days are numbered, by hearing of the arrival of the Scotia. God grant her next ocean voyage may be a safe, a prosperous, and a speedy one!

September 30th—Liverpool to Dublin.—Left the Prince's Dock about eleven o'clock, and crossed the Mersey to Birkenhead; from whence we journeyed to Hollyhead by rail, changing carriages at Chester. We caught sight of the grand tubular bridge—a great work of art, of which all the world has heard—and had an occasional glimpse of the mountains of Wales. About half-past two we left Hollyhead, and occupied about four hours in crossing St. George's Channel, arriving at the fine harbor o

Kingston at half-past six. Taking the train in waiting, in half an hour we were in Dublin; thus making the journey from England to Ireland in eight hours. After a late dinner at the Gresham Hotel, we strolled down Sackville Street, and crossed the Liffey.

October 1st—Sunday in Dublin.—At eleven o'clock, left the hotel to attend the *Presbyterian* church, Rutland Square; but learned that the service did not commence until the unusual hour of twelve. We then visited several other places of worship, but found that twelve was the customary hour, and concluded to return to Rutland Square. The squares through which we walked were strangely quiet, and the streets almost deserted. Being still much before the time, we had an opportunity of looking at the new and beautiful edifice itself. We learned, furthermore, that it was an old Scotch church, and that it had been erected chiefly through the liberality of one private gentleman. The service was simple, animated and impressive, such as one might expect to hear in this land of native eloquence. "If the Son shall make you free, ye shall be free indeed," was the text of the sermon, and it contained several apt and striking illustrations, some original and beautiful ones. He was not intending (said the minister) to speak of the freedom of some foreign body or nation, but *ourselves.* There was much counterfeit freedom. That of the maniac who twines together what rags he can find, and putting them upon his head, struts about in presence of his miserable companions, giving his orders and imagining himself a king, yet all the while casting sidelong glances at his keeper, of whom he stands in awe. So men stood in terror of God's judgments. As men in counsel are enabled by the telegraph to speak to one another, when far-distant from each other, as if but a curtain hung between them, so God's judgments are brought near to man by the human conscience ; so God's will and the world above is brought into instantaneous communication with the heart of man. Man in terror of these judgments is not aided in the onward course by a representation of greater punishment, but needs to be drawn by *love* to God—as a ship sailing into some foreign port, and, striking upon a rock, cannot be pulled off by any power, but may be easily loosened by the rising of a few feet in the tide. We are charged with sin, but we may be discharged.

In the afternoon went to the " Cemetery of Prospect," and walked through the grounds, some portions of which are tastefully arranged. Saw the O'Connell monument, and the coffin in which the remains of the great Irishman repose. It was painful to notice the requests upon the stones that the passer-by would pray for the deceased ; and we were struck with one quotation from the Apocrypha, declaring it to be " a good and wholesome thing to pray for the dead." Before returning " home," we drove to St. Patrick's Cathedral, an old building, recovered and rebuilt from and upon the remains of the former ancient edifice. It is truly a beautiful building, and contains, besides several monuments, (including a bust of Dean Swift, whose remains are here buried), a most exquisitely sculptured pulpit, representing several of the apostles, and the appropriate texts, " How shall they believe in whom they have not heard ? How shall they hear without a preacher ? How shall they preach except they be sent ?"

October 2d—Dublin.—This morning we read several columns in the daily paper on the "Fenian Agitation." The article affirms that the conspiracy is preventing tourists from visiting Ireland, and injuring the "Dublin International Exhibition." We found, however, in passing into the entrance hall of the Exhibition buildings, a goodly number of visitors, all of whom seemed to be much entertained with the display of sculpture, paintings, and wares peculiar to the nations from whence they came. Costly silks and bronzes from France; Russia leather and stag-ware from Russia; the interior of a Chinese house from China; skins and furs from Nova Scotia; magnificent carriages of all descriptions from England; and so forth. The Italian sculpture, chiefly from Rome, and pure and white as the native marble from which it had been cut, was very beautiful, and worthy the journey across the channel to see it. Among them were statues of Saul and Judith, by our countryman Mr. Story. There were not a few fine paintings, a number of which were the property of no less a personage than Queen Victoria. The reconciliation between Reynolds and Romney was peculiarly well executed, and the collection contained many paintings which we would be pleased to call our own. The grounds surrounding the palace are charmingly and handsomely arranged, and looked very inviting from the balconies. After selecting a few photographic views of the building itself, and a few of its treasures, and doing a limited amount of "shopping" in the arcades, we enjoyed a drive in Phœnix Park, a very extensive green, containing some seventeen hundred acres. There are not a few noble trees within the park, and pleasant rides several miles in length. Saw the Lord Lieutenant's and Lord Mayor's carriages while riding. The half hour devoted to the Zoological Gardens was very entertainingly spent. We saw the handsomest tiger in one of the cages that we had ever looked upon, and watched the animals while the keeper fed them with the raw and dripping carcass of some less fortunate quadruped. The collection is one of the finest in Europe, and deserving of a more lengthened and careful examination than we could bestow upon it. But we had yet to visit one or two of the large well-stocked dry-good stores, in order to secure some souvenir "from Ireland," to take to those whom we did not wish to forget, ere we made ready for the first and only night journey we have made during all our travels.

Friday, October 6th—Liverpool.—Our last day in the Old World has dawned, and its light has faded away! To-day we received our final salt-water letters, and have packed our trunks for the return voyage across the ocean. The last few days have been passed very quietly. Not that we have seen every thing which one might be interested in viewing in this city, nor because we have become satiated with sight-seeing. But there has come an unaccountable quietude upon our spirits—an undefinable hush—the cause of which we have not attempted to analyze. Perhaps it is induced by the thought that the travel which has been so fraught with deep pleasure, excitement, satisfaction, and profit, is at an end. Amongst the latest and best delineated pictures that we have seen is one entitled "From Waterloo to Paris." It represented Napoleon in the cabin of one of the abodes of the lower classes, seated before a blazing wood fire, wrapped in the sternest and most soul-absorbing meditations, while

the startled awe-struck owners of the hut are gazing at him
in astonishment, and carrying on a pantomimic conversation. It was a fascinating picture; and as the thoughts
connected with that bloody field of battle so engrossed
the mind of that mighty fallen general as to render him
oblivious to his own position, as well as to all that was
going on around him, so may it be that the recollection of
the sights we have seen, the sacred historic grounds upon
which we have trodden, has rendered our humble selves
scarce conscious of our situation, and heedless as to the
busy flow of life by which we have been so constantly
surrounded—not that we have any distinct remembrance
of any particular journey, or wonderful exhibition of
man's perseverance and genius. It is rather a realization
of a vast accumulation of images and thoughts, impressed
indelibly upon our minds, to be recalled and enjoyed when
time and distance shall have enabled us to meditate calmly
upon the past.

Sunday, October 8th—Off Queenstown.—We embarked
yesterday, under most favorable circumstances, about nine
and one-half o'clock, and were under way by half-past
eleven for America. The sun was warm and the water calm,
and we passed most of the day on deck. We came to anchor
at Queenstown before daylight this morning, and here we
have remained almost all day. About eleven, attended the
English Church service, conducted by Captain Judkins in
the large saloon, where by far the greater part of the passengers were assembled. The Captain's manner and aspect
was serious and agreeable, and the service well and heartily conducted. For a sermon, we listened to one of the
" Graver Thoughts of a Country Parson," and all joined

heartily in the prayer, written expressly for those upon
the sea—upon the bounding billows of which we were
soon to be tossing. About four, just as we sat down to
dinner, and in a storm, we left port. Owing to the
tide and the short sea, caused by the storm, there was
much motion; and between seven and eight o'clock not
a few were unmistakably sea-sick, and went to bed forgetting that it was Sunday—forgetting in a moment all
past pleasures, and in fact everything but their own
miserable selves.

October 9th.—Got out of our births about eight o'clock.
Sea-sickness gone; but owing to the heavy swell many of
us complain of an unpleasant sensation in our heads, as
if the upper portion of our craniums were about to part
company with the lower. We ate but a slim breakfast.
Spent most of the day on deck, reading, talking, and walking. Found a sheltered spot behind the wheel-house,
where we sat for a long time watching the waves, and
thinking of the unchangeable past; the uncertain present;
and the possible future. Wind " dead ahead." Making
thirteen knots per hour.

October 10th.—Sea much agitated. Uncomfortable remaining upon deck a part of the time. Wind still directly ahead. No sail seen all day. Many passengers sea-
sick. Those who are not affected, are many of them
quiet and moody. The Scotia's company, as to soci-
ability, is in striking contrast to that met with on
board the French ship Lafayette, during our out-
ward passage. We have several well-known merchant-
gentlemen, and bankers, of New York, on board; among
them, R. L. Stuart, William Butler Duncan, and Charles

14

Livermore. Brougham, the actor, is also a passenger, and has kept quite a company in a roar of laughter, this morning over Artemus Ward's travels.

October 12*th.*—Yesterday the sea was more quiet, and the ladies again appeared on deck. It is not the captain's fault that they are not always there, for he makes frequent tours among the births, striving to arouse the indolent and encourage the timid ones, and induce them to arise and get out into the invigorating salt air. To day we have had a storm, and all have been more or less confined to the cabins. Having neglected to go on board the Scotia the day before the sailing of the steamer from Liverpool, we failed to secure seats in the larger saloon; but we were in some respects fortunate, as it is more quiet and retired in the fore saloon, and there is not so much motion. At the end of one of the tables sits the son of the mayor of Liverpool, who is going to make his first visit to America. How we should like, were it possible, to experience (for a single moment) the impressions made upon the mind of an intelligent man by a first sight of our native land!

Saturday, October 14*th.*—For two days we have had a high sea. Wind southwest and west. Shipped several heavy seas. We have been seeing the " Stormy Atlantic" in all its terror, strength, and glory. Our ship appears like a toy in the wild waste of waters, and it seems at times as though the great surging waves *must* go over our heads rather than under the keel of our noble vessel. This evening the ship received a tremendous slap from a wave, which brought all who were in the forward cabin to their feet; many of whom thought that *something* had happened, most assuredly; but when they saw that the iron-bound monster went rushing on, ploughing the watery ridges, and throwing the masses of water to right and left, they were soon calmed, and felt greater confidence than ever in the "strong and stately vessel" that could "weather all disaster." And indeed it was a comfort to know that the steamer was as perfect as all the combined forces of "earth, air, fire and water" could make it. But it was a greater to trust in Him whom "even the winds and the sea obey," and who could at any time "still the tempest." The prospect is, that we shall have a long and unpropitious voyage.

Monday, October 16th.—Much speculation as to the time when we shall arrive. All wearied of the ship life, and, notwithstanding its "awful grandeur," of the ocean. Indeed Capt. Judkins himself informed us, a few evenings since, that although not *sea-sick*, he was himself *sick of the sea*, and talked of giving it up. But although ready to volunteer a remark now and then, our trusty captain is not so ready to be questioned; and when some one asked him as to the truth of a certain story about the Scotia's just grazing an iceberg during a recent passage, his only answer was, that there were "a great many stories in the newspapers."

October 18th.—More pleasant weather. Yesterday some of the voyagers who have been invisible during almost the entire passage, made their appearance for the first time at the table; and it is most cheering to see the tables filling up again. To-day we are only three hundred miles from New York! All on board much more cheerful and talkative, and conjecturing as to the exact hour of the ship's arrival in port. The saloons are very noisy; but all cannot sympathize with the noise and hilarity. Some few have been sick since the ship left Liverpool, and some have other causes for sadness; but all are greatly thankful that the voyage is about over, and well pleased to be nearing their homes.

Thursday, October, 19th, 1865—*America!*—Just as we awoke this morning the vessel was stopped, and a pilot came on board. Then we knew that we could not be far from land—our native land—our homes. Not many hours afterward we entered the noble bay of New York, and, as we passed the Narrows, saluted the Forts Hamilton and Columbus; and after having received the health-warden on board, steamed rapidly up to the pier at Jersey City, and the noble ship poured forth its human freight. A few moments more, and many who had been long separated were looking into each other's eyes, clasping each other's hands, embracing and kissing one another, and exhibiting all sorts of demonstrations of joy. But before all this took place—so inexorable is law, so supreme in its demands over all affection and feeling is business—that friends and relatives who were in sight of one another, were not allowed to meet until more than a hundred *mail bags* had been first carried off from the ship. Yet there were those, no doubt, who were as anxiously waiting for some of the letters contained in those leathern bags as we were to pass the barrier that prevented us from having the satisfaction of *touching* those whom we so loved and longed to greet. Although the moments seemed very long, they were but brief; and presently we were at liberty to seek our homes, there to render thanks to God, who, during all our travels in foreign lands, and amid the dangers of the deep, had kept us securely, blest us greatly, and returned us, at the end of the fourth month from the time of our departure, to our prized though desolated homes.

July 19*th*, 1866.—The eight months that have elapsed since we completed our return voyage across the Atlantic have brought with them many changes, and, as is to be expected in this life, some most sad ones. Some of us who were passengers on board the fine ship Lafayette have met together most unexpectedly and quite recently in the house of mourning, to pay a last tribute of regard to the memory of one whose bright inquiring mind, courteous manners, and promising youth, had won our hearts, and whose pleasing, companionable ways and conduct had augmented our enjoyment of that first unequalled sea voyage. Another, high in position, and who was at the time of our visit to the bright capital of his kingdom, in the possession of life and health—the King of Belgium—is no more. The Princess Helena has become the wife of Prince Christian. War is raging in Germany, so that the harbors are blockaded, and visitors from the Old World must needs be transported overland to Havre, in order that they may return to their homes. Vast improvements are progressing and have been completed in Paris, and the surface of the fine square of the *Champ de Mars* is being rapidly covered with light and elegant buildings, wherein is to be gathered the industry of all nations and the inhabitants of all lands. The coils of the Atlantic Cable are being again laid upon the mountains and across the valleys of the deep, and we may soon expect to read daily bulle-

tins from London, Paris, Vienna, and Constantinople!
So multitudinous, and various, and momentous are the
changes that are almost daily taking place in the great
arena of the world, that it would seem almost a folly to
write of the present, unless in view of its serving as history, in a few short months, or, at most, years—not only
physical, material changes, but those more powerful ones
of *mind*. Had Alexander the Great been a victor of the
world of mind, he need not have wept because more con-
quests were impossible, and he might have been Alexander the Great*est*.   God grant that all who have been
interested in watching the progress of those great events,
discoveries, and questions, which now interest the earnest,
thinking part of mankind, may live to see the significance
of those events made plain; those discoveries in practical
operation; and those vexing problems satisfactorily solved.
And yet may we all remember that the time cometh
apace when "those who weep will be as though they
wept not, and those that rejoice as though they rejoiced
not." and when "all knowledge shall vanish away."
Thankful for all those pleasures which may fall to our
lot, may we yet strive to understand the great mystery
of life, and so live that when the end of all things shall
come to us, we may fearlessly and resignedly go forth to
meet the future—life's duty done,